"Such a disappointing greeting for your husband,"

he murmured. "I had hoped for something a little more—familiar."

The way he said the word made it sound like an insult, and yet the lilting Italian accent sent a shiver of graphic remembrance through her in spite of herself. "You are my husband in name only," she stated. "We have been separated for over two years, and legally that means I am now free to seek a divorce. Surely you realize that, Stefano?"

There was a spark of anger in the dark, glittering eyes, but it was gone in seconds. "I realize it only too well, *cara*," he said. "But as you know, divorce means nothing to me. In the eyes of the church, and in—" he dropped his voice to a velvety whisper "—*my* eyes, we will always be man and wife, with all the endless and delightful possibilities that the state of matrimony offers."

SHARON KENDRICK started storytelling at the age of eleven and has never really stopped. She likes to write fast-paced, feel-good romances with heroes who are so sexy they'll make your toes curl!

Born in west London, she now lives in the beautiful city of Winchester—where she can see the cathedral from her window (but only if she stands on tiptoe). She has two children, Celia and Patrick. Her passions include music, books, cooking and eating—and drifting off into wonderful daydreams while she works out new plots!

Cruel Angel

SHARON KENDRICK

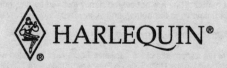

TORONTO • NEW YORK • LONDON
AMSTERDAM • PARIS • SYDNEY • HAMBURG
STOCKHOLM • ATHENS • TOKYO • MILAN • MADRID
PRAGUE • WARSAW • BUDAPEST • AUCKLAND

For Katrina, David, Claire and Jenny Hindmarsh, with love.

ISBN 0-373-80526-8

CRUEL ANGEL

First North American Publication 2002.

Copyright © 1993 by Sharon Kendrick.

This edition published by arrangement with Harlequin Books S.A.

Visit us at www.eHarlequin.com

Printed in U.S.A.

CHAPTER ONE

'Two minutes, Miss Carter.'

Cressida nervously smoothed clammy palms down her naked thighs, wishing that she could dispel her nerves.

Her costume didn't help, of course. The play was set in the late nineteen-fifties, the action taking place in a beach house, and for a large chunk of the time Cressida wore a swimsuit. True, with its ruched skirt, and its fairly innocuous wired bodice, it was hardly shocking, and, compared to some of the outfits you saw on the high street, positively innocent. But Cressida knew that there was something about seeing a partially clad woman on stage which drew far more attention than someone wearing something scanty in the street. It had been one of the first things she'd learnt at drama school—how the stage exaggerated, and gave emphasis—not just to emotions, but to costumes and scenery, too.

'You're on, Miss Carter.'

Her pulses were weak and flying, her heart hammering in her chest. She was paralysed. She would never move again from this spot. And then she heard her cue line, and she ran lightly on to stage right.

It was the pivotal moment of the play...the one where she discovered her husband's infidelity. Adrian, the actor playing her husband, was engrossed in a letter, but the sound of her footsteps disturbed him. He was to turn to her, and their eyes were to meet, and her expression was meant to convey the sudden realisation of the extent of his betrayal.

It was a difficult scene at the best of times, but today, in this stiflingly tense atmosphere, it needed every ounce of her professional skills to inject all the meaning which the playwright demanded. Just what was this tension? she wondered. She could almost smell it in the air, could feel it surrounding her like a heavy cloud, reminiscent of the charged, expectant air just before a storm broke.

It was unusual enough two weeks before opening to have a full dress rehearsal, and on stage instead of in the rehearsal rooms. Most of the cast had muttered about it, but Cressida had just put it down to one of the director's little foibles.

She briefly looked down towards the back of the house, to where Justin, the director, sat in his customary chair, but today, to her surprise, he was not alone. She could see the shadowy form of a man beside him.

She began speaking her lines, uttering them in the anguished way which was still comparatively easy for her to do. For who better could convey the despair and the loneliness of a marriage in its final death throes?

But she found the words unbearably difficult this afternoon. The atmosphere in the theatre was affecting her in a tangible way. She whirled to pick up the champagne glass to hurl at Adrian, and as she did her eye was caught by a movement next to the director. She stared into eyes that glittered like jet, and the plastic glass slipped out of her hand to bounce harmlessly at her feet. Her head bowed forward as if it were too heavy for her slender neck to support.

'Oh, my God,' she said weakly, and passed out.

When Cressida came round a few seconds later, it was to uproar all around, with Justin, the director, on his feet. 'What's going on?' he was shouting. 'See to her, someone!' then, holding his hands helplessly up in the air, as he turned to the tall black-haired man who stood beside him.

'I'm sorry about this; I don't know what's got into her. She must be ill.'

Cressida heard a horribly familiar voice—deep, with the slightest foreign inflexion.

'Ill?' The voice mocked. 'Indeed?'

With a monumental effort she forced her eyes open to find herself surrounded by her fellow actors—Jenna holding a glass of water and Adrian proffering a cool cloth. She pushed them away, determinedly getting to her feet, smiling at Adrian to indicate that she wished to continue with the scene.

'I'm fine,' she insisted. It had been an illusion, she thought desperately. It must have been. A flashback brought on by the content of the play. '*Fine*. Honestly!' She straightened her back as she stood up, giving her familiar wide-mouthed smile, which shrivelled and died like a scorched leaf when she saw that it had been no illusion. The man had risen, along with Justin, but he made the director fade into insignificance. He was staring at her intently, but the theatre was too dark to interpret the expression on his face. Not, she thought bitterly, that it had ever been a face which wore its feelings openly.

Her eyelids felt as if they had been weighted with

lead, fluttering to cover the huge eyes, and when she opened them again he had gone.

She was unable to carry on. It had never happened before, and she was close to tears. She had always been a professional, through and through, and now here she was, a quivering wreck, her hands shaking as if she had seen a ghost.

But you *have* seen a ghost, tormented a voice in her head. The ghost of your past. You had never thought to see him again; not now—after all this time. Hadn't she prayed for that, night after night, once her initial heartbreak was over?

Justin scrambled up on to the stage. He held out his hands and grasped hers tightly. 'Don't worry, lovie.' He smiled. 'Is it nerves, or are you ill?'

She gave a pale smile. 'Headache,' she said lamely. 'I'm sorry, Justin.'

Justin fished a peppermint out of his pocket and began to crunch. 'Go home,' he said firmly. 'And rest. You're my favourite actress, and you've never pulled a stunt like this before. We'll rehearse tomorrow instead. Now *go*! Quick! Before I change my mind!'

She wanted to ask him about the man sitting with him, about what he wanted with him. Or with her? But to ask that would be to acknowledge that she knew him, and that was the last thing she wanted. That was an area of her life which she had carefully concealed— a definite no-go area, and far too painful to resurrect.

She stumbled back to her dressing-room, collapsing into the chair in front of the mirror, her green eyes looking huge in her unnaturally white face, the full lips a ghastly slash of trembling scarlet.

Had she dreamed it? Could she just have imagined

it? An over-active imagination conjuring up an image of him? She shook her head, the hairspray-stiffened fifties hairstyle scarcely moving. That had been no dream. That had been Stefano, in the warm, living flesh.

And then it dawned on her. The letter from her solicitor had gone to his in Rome just a couple of months ago, requesting a divorce after two years of separation. And it had gone unanswered. Stefano had ignored it. 'Leave it for a while,' her solicitor had reassured her. 'There's often a hiccup at this stage. Cold feet, perhaps. Your husband may have decided he doesn't want a divorce, after all.'

Like hell, thought Cressida bitterly. An ultimatum delivered coldly, followed by absolute silence for two years. No further evidence was needed to convince her that Stefano wanted her out of his life.

She could remember the words he had used as if it had been yesterday. 'I will not have you remaining in England to work, while I am in Italy. A wife's place is by her husband's side, and if you take this job then our marriage is over.' But there had been no choice— she *had* to take it—that way lay sanity, at least. And what alternative had he offered her? A marriage growing worse by the minute with a cold, distant husband who seemed only to want her when she was in his bed?

Cressida stared sightlessly into the lighted mirror of her dressing-table, sitting as mute and as still as a statue. And in her heart she knew that she was waiting, so that when the knock came she didn't even start, but moved slowly towards the door as if she had been put on automatic pilot.

It could, of course, have been anyone—a member of the cast, the director, or the prompt: all legitimate visitors to see how she was feeling after her unexpected collapse. But she knew without a doubt that it was none of these. Even the knock at the door was typical of the man—not loud and insistent, but soft and firm, the trademark of a man who did not have to yell and bluster to get what he wanted. Oh, yes, she thought, that was Stefano to a T—used to getting exactly what he wanted in that quietly determined way of his.

She pulled the door open, carefully composing her face, knowing that polite disinterest would be her most effective weapon. 'Hello, Stefano,' she said coolly.

Black eyebrows arched arrogantly. 'Such a disappointing greeting for your husband,' he murmured. 'I had hoped for something a little more—familiar.'

The way he said the word made it sound like an insult, and yet the lilting Italian accent sent a shiver of graphic remembrance through her in spite of herself. She prayed for the right, dispassionate response. 'You are my husband in name only,' she stated. 'We have been separated for over two years and legally that means I am now free to seek a divorce. Surely you realise that, Stefano?'

She had a reaction at last. There was a spark of anger in the dark, glittering eyes, but it was gone in seconds. 'I realise it only too well, *cara*,' he said, in a voice which was soft with menace. 'But, as you know, divorce means nothing to me. In the eyes of the church—and in—' he dropped his voice to a velvety whisper '—*my* eyes, we will always be man and wife, with all the endless and delightful possibilities that the state of matrimony offers.'

He stood, lounging in the narrow doorway, as though he had every right to be there, his stance relaxed, though she knew him well enough to know that the muscles beneath the smooth brown skin were flexed and alert.

Outwardly, she thought, he had changed little. Perhaps the features were slightly more fined down, but not dramatically so. Even as a relatively young man, his face had held none of the softness of youth. The eyes, even then, had been hard, glittering and far-seeing, the beautiful mouth always distorted by its habitual cynical smile. She had never been able to imagine him as a happy and carefree little boy—always as the curt, calm man who knew exactly what he wanted. She looked into the implacable brown eyes, searching for some hint of why he was here, but she saw nothing, bar a flash of the only emotion she had allowed herself to remember. Desire.

She forced herself to remain calm. They were, after all, in the middle of a busy English city, in a theatre full of her colleagues. He might have succeeded in making her feel as though she were trapped in some derelict Italian mountain hut, miles away from civilisation, but she patently wasn't. Why, she had only to raise her voice, and any number of people would come running to her aid. And Stefano was a powerful and successful businessman—it wouldn't augur well for his professional or personal reputation if she started screaming her head off and the Press got hold of it. She could just imagine the field-day the newspapers would have with something like *that*.

The only problem being that he hadn't done anything which wasn't in any way totally above board. And he knew it. He was regarding her now with a look of infuriating amusement.

'You look so angry,' he mused. His tongue curved briefly over the perfect teeth which looked so brilliantly white against the olive skin. 'I love that look,' he whispered. 'Sometimes you used to look just like that before we…'

Her cheeks flared, and it was as much as she could do not to slap her hands over her ears. 'Shut up!' she spat at him, terrified that his words would make her picture what he had been about to describe. If she remembered that, she would no longer be in control. 'Whether or not you consider we are separated is your problem. It's a fact. We are. By English law.'

She steeled herself to ask him, 'Why are you here, Stefano?' She looked at him expectantly, but he said nothing.

The silence grew as the dark eyes swept slowly and deliberately down every inch of her body, at first dispassionately, but then they lingered on her breasts, at the soft swell which was emphasised by the pushed-up wire foundations of the swimsuit. The gaze moved down—she saw it alight with interest on the still flat line of her belly—and further down, dark eyes glinting as they stared very deliberately at the soft curves of her bare thighs.

Her cheeks stung with fire as she registered the insolence of the inspection. She responded with the kind of flip comment she knew he would detest. 'Seen enough?' she taunted.

The cynical mouth curved. 'I don't think so,' he

murmured. 'I don't think I've seen nearly enough. But these others…these…' Here he spat out a word in Italian, a word she had never heard before.

She raised her eyebrows. 'Sorry?' she said haughtily. 'I'm afraid you've lost me.'

His eyes narrowed. 'Perhaps you would call them voyeurs,' he hissed.

'Voyeurs?' she interrupted scornfully. 'What on earth are you talking about?'

'The audience,' he spat out. 'The ones who come to feast their eyes on you.'

She laughed aloud. 'Oh, come, come, Stefano—I'm hardly indecently clad.'

'Do you like it?' he asked suddenly, his voice dangerously soft.

Bewildered, she stared at him. 'Like what?'

'These men, in the audience—the ones who watch you, who look at you, who want you in their beds at night. Does it excite you? Does it?'

She made as if to turn away, but he stopped her with a light touch of her forearm which didn't fool her for a moment—she could feel the steely strength behind it.

'Does it?' he persisted. 'Do you like them to look at your…breasts?' She gasped as he reached out and almost idly moved his hand down to encircle and to cup one breast, moving it skilfully over the nipple, knowing through years of experience, and the instinct he had always possessed when it came to touching her body, how to imprison it there through pleasure alone. Her knees sagged, as the spirals of pleasure shot through her body like flames. It had been so long. So long…

He was not speaking now, as if he sensed that words would make reality intrude, his fingers speaking for him as they moved with sweet accuracy over the thin material of the swimsuit. He bent his head to kiss her neck, slowly and luxuriously, moving to suck gently and erotically on the lobe of her ear, and then at last possessing her mouth in such a way as to make her fleetingly, incredulously think that his need was as fierce as her own. And even while she despised her weakness, she gave herself up to that kiss, returning it with a long-suppressed hunger as though it were the last true thing in the world.

Even during the bad times—and there had been many of those—even the very worst times, he had always been able to do this to her—to extract this response from her. He had been her teacher, her tutor, her master. He had schooled her in the art of love, and he, only he, could do this to her.

He had begun speaking again. 'And here.' He moved his hand down to the soft flesh of her inner thighs. 'Do you like them looking at you here?' He moved his mouth to hers, speaking against it, so that she could feel the warm sweetness of his breath. He was deliberately insulting her, and yet he was making her so dizzy with longing that she had to grip on to the taut line of his shoulders, afraid that she might collapse into a heap at his feet. 'Do you think they would like to do what I am going to do to you? Do you?' And he slipped his fingers inside the swimsuit, to find her honeyed moistness, and she gave a strangled moan and flung her arms tightly around his neck.

'Stefano!' she cried brokenly into his shoulder, every vestige of reason gone, unable to relinquish one second of the sweet joy he was inflicting on her, her lips burying themselves helplessly into the soft shaft of his neck. 'Stefano—no! We mustn't. You know we mustn't.' It was a pathetic, half-hearted plea, and they both knew it.

He ceased the insistent movement of his hand, she was pushed away with a cool firmness, and she watched in total disbelief as he calmly walked over to the mirror above the washbasin, adjusted his tie, glanced at the expensive gold wristwatch and then at her, his eyes coolly mocking. 'Most assuredly we mustn't,' he agreed. 'I have a business meeting to attend to. A very important meeting—and one which gives precedence over what I believe you English call a "quickie".'

There was a second of shocked silence while her mind tried to assimilate what he had just said to her, and when she did her temper, fuelled by a deep self-loathing, erupted with a vengeance. With a cry she launched herself at him, her small hands beating ineffectually at the solid muscular wall of his chest.

'How dare you?' she demanded. 'How dare you do that?'

'What?' he asked softly.

'To come in here like that, and to—to—'

'To touch you?' he mocked. 'To kiss you? To make you move beneath my fingers—your body telling me how much you still want me, even now?'

'Why, you animal!' she cried. 'You low-down, no-good...'

He was laughing, soft mirth lighting his eyes, as he caught her hands and looked down at her as though she were a very naughty little girl. 'Ssh, *cara*,' he murmured. 'You should not call your husband all these names…'

'You won't be my husband very soon!' she howled in frustration. 'I keep telling you!'

'Tch, tch.' He made a clicking noise with his teeth. 'So stubborn. Stop worrying your beautiful little head. There is nothing wrong with wanting me to make love to you. It is perfectly natural.'

'I'd rather burn in hell!'

He continued calmly, as if she hadn't spoken, still with that confident smile on his mouth, the same spark of anticipation in the cold, glittering eyes. 'I know you want me, and I want you. But not now. Or here. I don't want it to be on the floor of your dressing-room, after so long. I want there to be a bed—a small bed will do, but a bed, most assuredly. And it will be all night. I'm going to make love to you all night.'

In a minute she would wake up, but while the nightmare was in progress she might as well have her say. 'You are *not* going to make love to me! Get that into your conceited head, Stefano. *You are not going to come anywhere near me, ever again*. We are finished. Kaput. *Finito*.'

He looked at her with resignation, then shrugged his shoulders in that typically Latin way that she'd once found so impossibly endearing. 'I still want you,' he said.

'Well, *tough*!' she retorted, remembering, as if clutching on to a lifeline, his curiously old-fashioned loathing of slang.

'And—' another shrug '—you know me well enough, *cara*, to know that I always get what I want.'

She wondered fleetingly what kind of sentence

she'd get for murder with *this* amount of provocation. 'Not this time, you rat!'

His eyes widened. 'I had forgotten just how much you could infuriate me. And, as I recall, there was only one sure way in which I could subdue your wildness.'

He made as if to move towards her, and she leapt back as if he were about to thrust a knife in her. If he touched her she would be lost.

'Get *out* of here!' she screamed, when there was a knock at the door. She closed her eyes in horror, then grabbed her kimono, pulling it over the bathing-suit and knotting the cummerbund tightly around her tiny waist. 'Now look what you've done,' she hissed.

An expression of sardonic amusement lit the dark eyes as he witnessed her obvious discomfiture, and he shrugged his shoulders. 'Surely you have had men in your dressing-room before now?' he mocked.

Cressida directed her blackest and filthiest look at him as she pulled open the door. It was Alexia, Harvey's—the producer's—secretary, her expression of irritated surprise fading immediately into a dazzling smile directed at Stefano.

'I thought I saw you come in here,' she pouted.

'Mr di Camilla just—er—wanted my—autograph,' butted in Cressida, knowing, even as she said it, just how ridiculous it sounded.

And Alexia's expression said it all—this man was not a stage-door johnny, hardly the type who would hang around asking actresses for their autographs. She turned china-blue eyes on him. 'Justin's waiting for you in the foyer,' she said, putting her head to one side slightly so that a wing of golden hair fell alluringly over one eye.

'Thank you,' said Stefano formally, and then inclined his head in Cressida's direction. 'And thank you so much for giving me your...time, and your—er—autograph.'

He had managed to make a simple sentence sound positively indecent, she thought furiously. 'Good*bye*,' snapped Cressida.

'*Addio*,' he murmured.

'I'll take you to Justin now,' gushed Alexia eagerly, but he shook his head.

'There is no need,' he said firmly. 'I know the way, and I am certain that you must have better things to do than to act as my guide.' He smiled.

As if he didn't know, thought Cressida, with an oddly painful pang, that Alexia would have stuck to his side all day like a parasite if he'd let her.

Both women watched as he moved away, the superbly cut loose Italian suit only emphasising the remarkably muscular body which it covered.

Alexia stared at Cressida curiously. 'Did he really want your autograph?' she asked disbelievingly.

'Yes,' muttered Cressida abruptly, thinking angrily that she still didn't know why he'd been here. And what business did he have with Justin?

The older girl had mischief in her voice. 'Strange then,' she said innocently, 'that you've got lipstick smudged all over your mouth!'

Giving a yelp of rage, Cressida grabbed a handful of tissues covered in cold cream and wiped her lips bare. She turned to Alexia reluctantly. 'Better?'

'Better. I take it you approve of our new angel?'

There was a long pause, and, not getting the expected response, she looked at Cressida enquiringly. 'Did you hear what I said?'

'Yes,' said Cressida slowly, 'I heard.' She had been thinking what an appropriate description of Stefano that was—yes, he had the face of an angel, a dark, mysterious angel. A cruel angel. But then the true meaning of the word sank in, with all its likely repercussions. 'Angel' was theatre slang for the financial backer of a play, with all the power and influence which that position merited.

She stared at Alexia in disbelief.

'Oh, yes,' said Alexia chattily. 'I *thought* that you hadn't taken it in. He's been having hush-hush talks with Justin for weeks now—because the other backers are dropping out. He's a hugely rich Italian businessman, I gather—or perhaps you knew that already?' she fished.

'Why should I?' asked Cressida guilelessly, amazed at the ease of her lie and hating herself for it, and yet not seeing any alternative.

Why? she thought helplessly. Why is he doing it? Stefano had never been involved in the arts before— the very opposite, in fact. She asked herself the question without really wishing to know the answer.

She wasn't aware of the journey back to the flat, only of the taxi driver's startled expression when he took in her half-made-up face and the stiff, lacquered hair-do. He looked as if he was about to make a joke, but something in her expression must have stopped him, and the journey home was completed in silence.

All she knew was that she found herself lying on her bed, tears staining the thick foundation on to the cotton pillow, her dinner date with David forgotten.

Crying, not because fate had brought Stefano back into her life, but because he represented a happier time, the time of her life, and she was reminded with heart-rending clarity of how it had once been between them, such a long time ago...

CHAPTER TWO

IT HAD been the second hottest summer that century, and England seemed to have caved to a standstill. Everywhere the atmosphere was still and heavy as lead. Even breathing seemed to take the most enormous effort, thought Cressida, as she sucked the hot air down into her lungs.

She was walking towards the park, having arranged to meet Judy her flatmate from the drama school at which they were both final-year students. No one went into the canteen or to cafés in weather like this—they sought the shelter of the frazzled trees, or the light breeze which they prayed they might find near the large pond.

Cressida saw Judy in the distance, gave a languid wave, and walked towards her. Her dark red hair was already damp around her temples, the thin material of her cotton dress limp with the heat and clinging to her body like a second skin. She wore a wide-brimmed straw hat—not, as so many of her peers did, for effect, but because it protected the fair skin which had remained pale all summer.

She reached Judy, who was lying on a beach towel spread out on the grass. She sat up and smiled as Cressida approached.

'Hiya, Cress!' she called. 'Come and eat—I've

made heaps of sandwiches. Ham and tomato, egg and cress. *Cress*! Get it?!'

Cressida's shaded eyes were raised heavenwards. 'Original sort of person, aren't you?' she teased, and shook away the foil-wrapped packages which her friend offered, wrinkling her nose at them. 'No, thanks. I couldn't face them. I don't know how you can eat in this sort of weather.'

'Oh, you just want to be thin, thin, *thin*,' teased Judy as she flapped her hand in the air. 'Go away!' She swiped again. 'Bother these wasps—there's millions of them.'

'Well, if you buy jam doughnuts, what do you expect?' asked Cressida drily, and sank down on to the grass, pulling off the straw hat, so that her hair tumbled down the sides of her face.

Judy's sandwich froze in mid-air. 'Wow!' she breathed. 'Hot!'

'Too much mustard?' enquired Cressida mildly.

'Hotter than that. I'm in love!'

'Where?'

'Over there. Don't look now. Oh, *Cressida*—now he'll see!'

And Cressida saw him.

He was sitting across the grass from them, but his face was clearly visible. The thing that struck her first was how cool he looked, and how surprising that was in view of the fact that he was wearing more clothes than almost anyone else. Not for him the ubiquitous uniform of singlet and shorts—a lot of them worn by pot-bellied men who should have known better. This man was wearing a lightweight suit of cream, against which his olive skin contrasted superbly well. She

She leaned closer into the table. "Sometimes we need to see the beauty in creativity, just like we need to see the good in the worst of people. You act as though your way is the only way things ought to be done."

"It's the best way."

"Excellence knows no master."

He instantly raised a brow. "Mother, you're quoting Plato."

"Yes, *The Republic,* book ten. I can read, you know." She sat straighter and stirred her coffee. "Mark my word, *mi hijo,* you will have an ulcer by the time you're thirty and heart problems by the time you're thirty-five if you don't find the beauty in life."

Carlos felt frustration seep through his skin. In his estimation, an undisciplined life had a lot to do with his mother's diabetes and his father's untimely death due to alcoholism. He intended to lead a healthy, ordered life, with God's help of course.

"And furthermore, I would appreciate it if you would stop by to see your mother because you love her, not because you're checking to see if she's following her diet and taking her medication."

three

Carlos nearly choked on his cake. "I do love you, Mother, which is why I want to make sure you're taking good care of yourself. Guess I could have been a little more discreet, but you don't do what the doctor mandates."

She shook her head and pursed her lips. "No child of mine is going to be saddled with looking after me. I refuse to be a burden."

"You are not—"

"I'm not finished yet," she said, instantly silencing him as she narrowed her gaze. "Now, why haven't you applied to Harvard? Wouldn't a degree from there establish your credibility as a politician?"

"I hadn't looked into it," he said sheepishly.

"Then do it," she said and accented her words with a sweet smile. "Now, let's finish our meal. So when are you taking the leather goods to the boutique?"

Carlos left his mother's home shortly after eight-thirty. The comment she made about his habits bothered him. In the past, she'd defended him when others made fun of or criticized his mannerisms. Tonight she'd surprised him, and he wondered if his habits had grown worse as he worked toward his goal of ordered, disciplined living. *Maybe I'm getting old. After all, I'm twenty-four; next year my car insurance premium goes down.* He shifted in his truck seat, and wiped away a piece of invisible dust on the dashboard, then flipped on the overhead light to ensure his hair looked good.

His orderly environment suited him fine. Someday he'd be asking people to vote him into public office. They'd need to rely on a man whose feet were firmly rooted in Christ and found herself studying him closely, which in itself was unusual, thinking to herself that he, of all people, would have looked superb in some of the sawn-off denims which were all the rage that summer. The man had loosened his tie, and that was his sole concession to the day.

Dark brown velvet eyes met hers, and held them in a mocking gaze, one eyebrow raised in question, and she hurriedly looked away, taking a mouthful of the warm lemon barley beside her.

'I didn't get a look-in,' said Judy in mock disgust. 'He was too busy ogling you.'

Cressida blushed. 'He wasn't really.'

'Yes, he was.' Judy finished the last of her sandwich and rolled over on to her stomach. 'Oh, well—I might as well tan the back of my legs. Do you want some cream?'

Cressida shook her head from side to side, trying to create some moving air, but it was no good. There was simply no cool to be found. 'No, thanks—I'll burn. I want some shade. I'll wander down towards the lake.' She stood up, in a fluid movement which was testimony to the years of ballet training. She tucked her copy of *Antony and Cleopatra* under her arm, and slowly walked across the fried earth.

She had found the welcome green umbrella of a horse-chestnut, when she heard a loud buzzing and a wasp danced infuriatingly around her face. She waved it away. 'Off! *Off*!'

But the wasp was persistent, straying so dangerously close to her eye that her wild swipe at it sent her off balance, causing her to trip forward, one foot catching the jagged edge of an exposed tree root.

Down she tumbled to sit on the grass, seeing the sudden appearance of blood on her foot. The pain brought tears to her eyes, and as a shadow moved over her she looked up with over-bright eyes at the man in the suit.

'Do not cry,' he said gently, and she noticed that his voice had the slightest foreign inflexion. 'Here. Let me see.'

And, before she could stop him, he had crouched beside her, gently removing her sandal and putting it aside, and then he was cradling her foot in the palm of his hands, examining it with long fingers which were both cool and firm. Bizarrely, she felt an electric tingling at the curiously intimate sensation of his skin touching hers, and in an automatic reflex she tried to withdraw the foot.

'No, please...' she protested without conviction, her normal *savoir-faire* deserting her. She was transformed instead into a creature who was gazing up at him as if he could take the pain away by magic.

'Yes,' he insisted quietly. 'I will dress it for you.'

She watched as he retreated to the tree where he'd been sitting to pick up a bottle of mineral water. He saw her bemused expression as he returned. 'Not fizzy,' he smiled. 'Still water. And Italian—so it's only the best, naturally, for such an exquisite foot!'

Involuntarily, she gave a slight shiver at the compliment he paid her, watching as he tipped the mineral water over a fine piece of linen which he produced from his jacket. He squeezed it out with strong hands and then, very firmly, tied it around her narrow foot.

The coolness of the makeshift bandage provided instant relief, but, perversely, she missed that contact with his hand as he had touched her bare flesh. She found herself looking at the line of his mouth, at the slightly mocking upward curve at each side—and began to wonder what it would be like to be kissed by him.

She shook her head to make the thoughts go away. Crazy thoughts! Summer madness. Heat-stroke. 'I have to go,' she said.

To her surprise he made no demur. He nodded. 'Of course.' And with the same delicate touch he slipped her bare foot back into the sandal, his dark eyes narrowed slightly as they looked at her with concern. Prince Charming, she thought suddenly, as he fastened the strap.

He sprang like a panther to his feet and, looking down at her, extended his hands.

She found herself reaching up her hands, and when he had grasped them he swung her up lightly so that she stood in front of him, looking up expectantly into his face. For a moment he frowned. He was very close. She could hear the humming of bees, and the longed-for breeze had just started. Her lips instinctively parted, and her green eyes were huge in her face.

And suddenly, he became very formal. 'Can you walk?' he asked courteously.

She felt as though she had snapped out of a dream. 'Yes, I'm fine,' she said, very shaken, though less by the accident than by the realisation that she had been standing waiting to be kissed by a man who was a total stranger to her. And thank God, she thought, that he had not responded. She tried to move away, but he caught her by the elbow.

'Let me help you,' he insisted, in that mocking, accented voice, and slid his arm around her slender waist to walk her back to Judy.

And she allowed him to hold her in that familiar way, relaxing naturally against his strength. The short journey was heaven, but, too soon, they'd arrived. She saw Judy roll over from her prone position, rubbing her eyes, her expression of curiosity showing that she'd seen nothing of the incident. 'I—tripped,' Cressida explained, still weak from the effect that this man was having on her.

His hand dropped from her waist. 'It will cause you pain for no more than a few hours, I think.' He smiled. And then he looked down at a mute Cressida, cupping her chin between thumb and forefinger. '*Ciao*,' he said softly, so softly that only she could hear, and then he walked away over the brown grass, the brilliant sunlight glancing off the dark hair.

There was silence for a moment. Judy's eyes were like saucers.

'Who *was* he?' she demanded. 'Close-up he's even more of a hunk!'

It sounded absurd, even to Cressida. 'I don't know,' she admitted.

'What do you mean—you don't know?' quizzed Judy.

'Just what I say,' replied Cressida, a touch querulously. 'I've never seen him before in my life, and all I know is that he tended to my foot.' Her eye was caught by the linen handkerchief.

'But did you see the way he was looking at you? Did you give him your phone number?'

'He didn't ask,' said Cressida, trying, and failing, to sound annoyed at the implication that she might give out her phone number to a person she had just met. Because if she were perfectly honest, she would have given it—willingly.

Judy was looking at his retreating back-view just visible in the distance. 'Well, that's that, then. London's a big place—you'll never see him again.'

And that was what Cressida had thought, too, after a week of spinning 'What if?' fantasies.

What if he went there for lunch every day? Would it look too obvious if she went back there? And why should it? she reasoned—for all he knew it might be *her* regular lunchtime venue. Which might have been all very well in theory, had the weather not broken with a series of alarming thunderstorms which prevented her from re-visiting the park.

What if he worked near the drama school? Along with half a million others, she thought wryly. If he *did* work near by, she never saw him, even though she spent too much of her meagre grant on frequenting the many swish new sandwich bars in the vicinity, thinking she might spot him.

No, she decided, as she pushed the fine linen handkerchief she had carefully laundered and ironed to the back of her underwear drawer—it had just been a strange, one-off encounter, and she should take comfort from the fact that she had reacted so strongly to him, stranger or not, because hadn't it worried her for long enough that she had seemed to share none of her peers' urges for sexual experimentation? Hadn't there been shrugs and whispered comments because she showed not the slightest inclination to disappear at parties—unlike the other girls, who were seen leaving the room with their current flames, usually in the direction of the bedroom.

A week went by, and, if not exactly *forgetting* about the man, then at least Cressida had put him out of her mind as she concentrated for the end-of-term production, in which she was playing Cleopatra.

It was a gruelling rehearsal, and she was glad enough to finish, sitting in the cramped dressing-room cleaning her face and trying to decide whether or not to go to her speech coach's party that night. But she was strangely reluctant. And let's face it, she thought, as she dragged the brush through her thick red hair— it'll be the same old faces, the same old jokes. No one will notice if you aren't there.

A long bath, a cool drink on the plant-filled patio and the flat to herself seemed an infinitely preferable option.

It was a warm, balmy night, with the setting sun gilding the clouds pink as she walked the short distance to the flat. She had been lucky to have hit it off with Judy so well in their first few weeks of term, and had been delighted to be asked to share the flat with her. Judy's parents were rich. Rich, rich, *rich*, as she cheerfully admitted herself. And they loved indulging their only daughter—thus the spacious flat in a prestigious area of London. Otherwise, Cressida—with her elderly aunt her only relation in England—would have been living in some grotty little flat, goodness knew where.

Her only bone of contention was that Judy had refused point-blank to accept any rent money. 'My parents have already paid for it,' she had pointed out. The only way round this was for Cressida to buy new things for the flat—so that every month a new vase, pretty dishes or colourful scatter cushions were introduced into their home.

Cressida had her bath, and pulled on a filmy wrap patterned in soft shades of green. Her hair dried into a cloud of fragrant dark waves shot with fire. She had just poured herself a glass of weak Pimm's and added lemon and a sprig of mint when there was a ring at the doorbell.

It must be Judy, she thought, back early and disenchanted by the party, but she opened the door to find the man from the park there, silently watching her, not a flicker of emotion on the implacable olive-skinned face.

She opened her mouth to say all the things which she knew one should say in such circumstances, from, 'What are you doing here?' to, 'How did you find out where I lived?' But she said none of these, just stood regarding him with the same intense interest as she saw reflected in his own eyes.

There was a mocking look in the quizzical way in which he surveyed her, one dark eyebrow arched, the trace of a smile touching the firm mouth. 'You knew I would come.'

She looked into those dark velvety eyes and was lost. She nodded. 'Yes,' she said, dry-mouthed, recognising the truth in his words immediately. 'I knew.' And, without another word, he had taken her in his arms and begun to kiss her.

Cressida groaned as she turned her head away from the pillow and lay staring at the wall. She had been so *young*, so naïve. Anyone who had ever doubted the veracity of the phrase 'she was like putty in his hands' had only to look at her relationship with Stefano.

She sat up, her hand going to her hair and encountering the thick lacquer which clogged it, her eyes going to the small clock on the rickety bedside table. It was gone seven, and David was due here at eight—and she hadn't even cleaned her face properly. If she didn't remove the heavy stage make-up soon, there would be hell to pay with her skin. Her head had begun to throb alarmingly. The last thing she felt like doing was going out to dinner, being forced to make polite conversation—even with someone as charming as David—not when her mind was spinning round like a Ferris wheel gone crazy.

She dialled his number with a shaky hand, and to her relief it was answered on the second ring. At least he hadn't already left.

'Hello, David—it's me, Cressida!'

'Well—hello to my favourite actress!' came the cheery reply. 'Are we still on for tonight?'

'I wondered,' she said apologetically, 'if I could take a rain-check?'

The cultured voice sounded anxious. 'You're not ill, are you?'

She liked him—she owed him more than a flimsy excuse, but not the truth; she couldn't face that. 'No, I'm not ill. It was just a—hard day. Tough rehearsal—you know.'

The anxiousness in his voice was magnified. 'Everything going all right with the play, I hope?'

She hastened to reassure him. 'The play's *fine*—you know it is. Hasn't everyone said that you're the best playwright since—?'

'I know. Since Shakespeare. Just not so prolific, nor so acclaimed.' He sighed. 'I've been looking forward to a date with my favourite actress all week, and now she's turning me down for no reason other than it's been a long day. I've had a long day, too, you know.'

'Oh, David—don't make me feel bad. It isn't that I don't want to see you—just that I don't feel up to going out for dinner.'

'Then we won't!' he said, sounding triumphant. 'And if Cressida won't go out to the restaurant then the restaurant must come to Cressida. We could eat a take-away—no problem. What do you fancy? Indian? Chinese? Pizza?'

'Oh, no—honestly. I wouldn't want to put you to any trouble.'

'It's no trouble,' he insisted.

She was fighting a losing battle here. 'But I'm not feeling very good company tonight.'

'You're always good company to me, Cressida,' he said quietly.

And after that declaration, she found it impossible to say no to him, agreeing that she would see him at eight-thirty, and that they would choose what they wanted from a local restaurant, and he'd go out to buy the meal.

As she replaced the receiver, she thought how ironic it was that David should make his first hint at something approaching seriousness at precisely the wrong time. They had been dating now for almost four months, and he was the first man she'd seen regularly since Stefano. The only man, apart from Stefano, she realised.

It had taken a long time for her to even consider

going out with another man after the breakup of her marriage, but David had seemed the perfect partner, the balm she needed to soothe her troubled spirit. He was everything she liked and respected in a man—and everything that Stefano was not. They liked the same things—primarily the theatre, but they also liked loading up their bicycles on to the roof-rack of David's estate car and escaping from the rat race into the country, where Cressida would sit quietly reading, while David indulged his hobby of photographing birds. Most importantly for her, everything they did did not end up with them in bed together. Her face flamed, and a pulse began to throb insistently as she recalled Stefano's idea of recreation. David was a gentleman. He was prepared to wait. But then a memory intruded—jarred and disturbed her—because so, too, had Stefano—at the beginning...

His kiss was like nothing she had ever experienced, on or off the stage. There had been no one special in her life—and at just nineteen that hadn't been so very unusual. And even the on-stage embraces, where the current breed of up-and-coming actors prided themselves on simulating realism, kissing you with an intimacy that Cressida had found slightly repugnant and definitely unnecessary—none of them had even remotely resembled what this man was now doing to her.

His mouth cajoled her into instant response, so that she found herself somehow knowing that he wanted their tongues to lace together in erotic dance—the result of which sent her heart-rate soaring, and made her insides melt. She felt a tingling awareness in the tips of her breasts, a growing warmth in her groin. She found that she wanted to explore the substance of his taut, muscular body, so that when he pushed her up against the wall and ground his hips into hers, like a man who was out of control, she did not cry out her protest, but urged him on with a slurred and exultant, 'Yes, oh, *yes*,' and his answer was to lightly brush his hands over her breasts, gently stroking each one in turn until he had her almost collapsing against him in agonised arousal, which was replaced with an equally agonised frustration when he suddenly stopped, his hands leaving her, but he himself not moving, just surveying her with dark eyes in whose depths were sparks she could not fathom.

He did not speak for a moment. Months later, he was to tell her that it was the first time in his life he had ever been rendered speechless. And when he did speak, it was with a rigid control which astounded her.

'Not now.' He shook his head. 'And not in such a way. If you had not been wearing such a garment—' he shrugged in the direction of the filmy green wrap '—then I should not have lost my head.' He lowered his voice. 'When I collect you tomorrow—at eight— you will wear something more—' he seemed to muse for a second, and then he smiled, a smile which transformed the handsome, stern face into someone she knew she would die for '—suitable. Cover up a little, yes? Or I will not be responsible for my actions, *cara*. But not trousers. Promise me you will never cover up your legs with trousers?'

It was preposterous, but she found herself agreeing in delight, loving the mastery in his voice as he spoke. Had she been older, wiser, surely she would have steered clear of a man who, even at that early stage, had shown such a strong inclination to control her?

He was turning to leave, his hand on the door-handle, when something shocking had occurred to her. 'Your—your name?' she stammered. 'I don't even know your name.'

He gave her a long, unbelievably sexy smile, before leaning forward to plant on her mouth a slow kiss of such unbearably sweet promise that she trembled again. 'Names are not important,' he murmured. 'But it is Stefano. Stefano di Camilla.'

She liked it, loved the way he said it. It had an imperious ring to it. Her green eyes widened as she replied, almost shyly—and this in itself was strange, for she was never shy as a rule. 'And I'm Cressida,' she said. 'Cressida Carter.'

'I know.' His voice was soft. 'You see, I know everything about you.'

Cressida closed her eyes as she stood beneath the piercingly cold jets of the shower, remembering how flattered she had been by his research. It seemed that he *had* gone to a great deal of trouble to find out about her. Somehow, he had tracked down where she lived, and with whom, and where she studied—and what. He had even discovered that her parents had followed the dictates of the late sixties, and had 'dropped out'—living in splendid if somewhat basic isolation on the Balearic Island of Ibiza. She remembered running her fingers wonderingly through the thick, springy hair, and asking him how he had learnt so much about her in such a short time, but he had shrugged nonchalantly, and kissed away her questions, telling her that things like that were of no consequence to her.

What he had meant, of course, she thought grimly as she massaged more shampoo into her scalp to attempt to remove the stubborn lacquer, what he had *meant* was that she shouldn't bother her pretty little head about things which didn't concern her. For wasn't that one of the maxims by which the di Camilla family lived—that women should just sit quietly and beautifully in the background, providing comfort and satisfaction for their men?

Cressida shook her wet hair as she stepped out of the shower and began to rub herself dry, her pale skin glowing with the friction of the rough towel. She pulled on a short cream satin dressing-gown and sat in front of the mirror at her dressing-table, the hairdrier blowing the dark red waves into angry fronds which echoed her mood, when there was a loud shrilling of the doorbell. Her brow creased momentarily. David, of course. He *was* early. Well, he would just have to wait in the sitting-room while she changed.

She ran lightly to the door, and pulled it open, the welcoming expression on her face dying immediately when she saw who it was who stood there.

'No,' she whispered disbelievingly.

'Oh, yes,' he contradicted softly, and then his eyes moved down, lingering slowly on the satin of her wrap, as he surveyed the fullness of her breasts which were tingling uncomfortably under his gaze—she could feel the taut peaks pushing against the silky material, and she automatically crossed her arms around her chest, shielding her betraying body from his gaze.

And the movement caused the hard line of his mouth
to twist in derision.

'I see you still answer the door as alluringly as possible,' he said harshly.

As he stared directly into her eyes, her imagination
stupidly led her to think that she saw a flash of some
deeper emotion than plain desire, a softening of the
harsh mouth, but it was gone before she remembered
that it had been a common fault of hers—crediting him
with feelings which he did not possess. She hugged
herself tighter as she looked down at the carpet, a lump
in her throat, willing the idiotic tears not to spring to
life.

'Tell me, do you always dress to please, Cressida?'

His words were a grim challenge and her eyes were
drawn unwillingly to his face. Sometimes she had
wondered if he was made of flesh and blood as she
was, and now she wondered anew. How could a face
which could move with such animation, which could
dissolve so sweetly with passion—how could such a
face remain now as cold and as unreadable as a blank
book? And yet she could still look on it and remember
how much she had loved him.

The sharp reminder of her lost love pierced her heart
like a sabre cut and, afraid that he would see and taunt
her moment of weakness, she moved a step away.
'You've got no right to come in here and criticise
me—and you'll have to go,' she said desperately. 'I'm
expecting—' she made her voice linger fondly
'—someone.'

That did it. She saw his muscles tense and a pulse
at his temple begin an ominous throbbing.

'And who is the lucky man?' he ground out. 'Do

you always greet him like—*this*?' His hand moved disdainfully as he gestured at the skimpy garment which covered her body. 'Is it the dear David—the man who writes these plays which no one can understand?'

'His plays are *wonderful*!' she defended shrilly, and she saw his mocking smile and knew that she had fallen into some kind of trap. She leaned forward angrily. 'And how did you know that I was seeing David? I suppose you've had all your nasty little spies out, haven't you? I forget that you have a whole network of information gatherers to do your dirty work for you.'

He returned her angry look with one of infuriating calmness, which did not fool her for a minute. 'From what I have seen of him, he does not look man enough to share your bed,' he goaded.

Knowing that she had a weapon which would wound his pride more than anything—she used it. 'He's man enough,' she retaliated.

For a moment she thought she had gone too far. She honestly thought that he was going to hit her—Stefano, who had never hit a person in his life before. She felt like shrinking away from the clenched fists at his side, their knuckles white with the restraint he was obviously exercising. She must have been mad to suggest to him that David was her lover, when he was due to arrive at any minute, and knowing Stefano's fiercely possessive pride. She couldn't repress a small shudder as she imagined an angry confrontation. And then, surprisingly, she saw his stance relax, and he walked straight past her to stroll into the sitting-room. She followed him in frustration.

When he turned round, all traces of his anger had disappeared, to be replaced with an expression of disdain. He stared incredulously at the small room, at the shabby furniture, the clean but well-worn curtains. 'You live like *this*?' he said scornfully. 'Is this what you broke up our marriage for—to live like *this*! Like a—pauper?'

'I *like* this flat,' she defended. 'And at least it's mine. Paid for by me.'

'It is not a suitable place for my wife to live,' he said flatly.

Her temper was on the verge of eruption. 'How many times do I have to tell you before you get it into your stubborn head? I am your wife in name only— and not for very much longer, thank God!'

'We will see how much of a wife you are.' He smiled infuriatingly.

That sounded ominously like a threat, she thought, but even if it was he no longer had a hold on her. 'We could stand here scrapping all night, Stefano, but it won't change anything,' she told him with a studiedly cool assurance she was far from feeling. 'Why don't we just accept the fact of our incompatibility, and put it down to experience?'

'Experience?' he echoed softly. 'Is that what life is all about to you, Cressida, mmmm? A series of experiences to be lived through? To be discarded when it falls short of perfection? Is that why you ran away? In search of pastures new? Different and better—' his voice was harsh '''—experiences''?'

Her anger and her indignation were swallowed up by an inexorable sorrow. She had carefully and deliberately closed off that section of her life, had refused to dwell on the heartache he had inflicted on her when he had told her to go. And now it was as if he had ripped open her carefully healed wound, left her heart exposed and helpless.

She swallowed convulsively. 'We both know why I left.' She forced a quiet dignity into her voice. 'And I don't intend discussing it now. Just tell me one thing. Why have you come here?' She felt in urgent need of a good, strong drink, but she didn't dare get herself one. Stefano, a man never in need of any artificial stimuli, might interpret that as yet another weakness in her resolve, and hadn't she already betrayed enough weakness before him today to last a lifetime? 'Why have you come back?' she repeated.

He smiled enigmatically. 'There are a number of reasons.'

She felt as though she were playing a game of poker. 'Such as?'

'Perhaps I have revised my opinion of the arts—'

'Don't give me that!' she interrupted hotly. 'Why change the habits of a lifetime?'

'Or perhaps,' he continued, unperturbed, 'I see the play as a good investment.'

She let out a pent-up sigh. Of course! As easy as that. Profit. She should have guessed. He had riches to rival Croesus, but still it wasn't enough. In business, as in life, Stefano had a killer instinct. Life to him was just a series of deals to be made, possessions to acquire, then lock away. She'd been one herself, hadn't she? And thank God she'd got out in time. She looked at him with scorn. 'You're backing the play even though you've openly admitted you don't like it!' she accused.

'It is not to my taste.' He shrugged. 'But perhaps audiences are not quite so discerning.'

She found herself in the strange position of acting as David's champion. If only Stefano knew of the fundamental innocence of their relationship! 'The audiences are going to lap it up—because it comes from the heart. David believes integrity to be more important than profit,' she said coldly. 'Although it's a word I doubt whether you'd find in *your* vocabulary.'

He made a small sound of disgust underneath his breath. 'Integrity does not buy bread.'

Cressida suddenly felt very tired. This conversation was going precisely nowhere. When Stefano was in this kind of mood there was no arguing with him, and besides, David would be here at any moment, and the last thing she wanted was a confrontation. 'Will you please go now?'

In direct opposition to her request, he seated himself in one of the over-stuffed armchairs.

'Don't bother making yourself comfortable,' she snapped. 'I don't know why you're here, Stefano—all I *do* know is that I want to be left in peace to get on with my life. And I want you out of here. Is that clear?'

He ignored her question. 'And the company—do they know of their leading lady's relationship with their new backer? "Angel", I think you say.'

Fear dried her mouth. 'Of course they don't. No one knows...'

'No one knows we are married.' His voice was distorted with anger. 'Of that I am only too aware. Cressida wishes to be single again and *dunque*!' He snapped his fingers. 'Her wish shall be granted. This is a society where the vows of matrimony can be shrugged aside as casually as if they were of no consequence.'

'That isn't true!' she flared. 'There are reasons why I'm divorcing you—perfectly legitimate ones. And what is more I don't want anyone—*anyone*—knowing of my past relationship with you.'

The dark eyes glinted. 'Oh? And why is that?'

Her temper erupted. 'Oh, don't pretend to be so naïve, Stefano! My position would be intolerable! If any of them knew I'd been your wife, I'd be viewed with suspicion. I'd no longer be treated as an equal, would I?'

His mouth twisted. 'And yet you do not mind it being known that you are dating the playwright?'

'That's different, and you know it!' she exploded. 'You're backing it—you're providing the money. And money is power—as you are perfectly well aware.'

He had got to his feet in a single, light movement, the grace of which only emphasised the powerful strength of his tall frame. He stood studying her through hooded eyes which told her nothing. 'Very well,' he said. 'I will agree to keep our liaison quiet— on the condition that you have dinner with me tonight.'

Cressida felt like pinching herself to check that this was really happening. 'I can't have dinner with you. I've already told you—I'm expecting David.'

He gave a ruthless smile. 'Then we will take him, too.'

An involuntary shiver ran up her spine. Stefano sounding reasonable like this was Stefano at his most dangerous. 'What are you saying?' she demanded, her voice breaking on the question. 'What do you want?'

He shrugged. 'That is the thing to do in this country, is it not? The *"civilised"* thing? The husband and the wife who have once shared their lives to sit having dinner with the new partner. Did you not once tell me that you wanted it to be an amicable divorce?'

She looked at him helplessly, remembering the stumbling letter she had written to him after six months of separation—another letter he had ignored. Had she really been so naïve as to say that to him? 'What do you want?' she repeated weakly.

'I told you. Have dinner with me tonight, and our little secret will remain just that.'

The doorbell pealed, not as loudly as when he had pressed it, but loud enough to shatter the fraught silence.

Stefano smiled, his eyes roving in a lazy line from her bare toes to the curve of her hips where the satin clung. 'It is your choice, my beauty—so choose.'

She was trapped, she realised, as her wide green eyes stared at his implacable face. She should just tell him to go to hell and be done with it. But Stefano was not the kind of man to heed such a demand. And, apart from compromising her neutral position as one of the players in a very tight-knit company, if word of her marriage to Stefano got out, could she really bear the gossip, the surmising, the endless questions? If her marriage was laid bare for general analysis, then wouldn't it just force her to confront its failure herself? To remind her with heart-rending poignancy just how destroyed she had felt at its end?

The doorbell rang again.

'Well, beauty,' he murmured softly, 'have you decided?'

'Yes, damn you. Yes. The answer's yes.'

CHAPTER THREE

THE instant she had made her decision, Cressida began to regret it. As she opened the door to David, she wondered what possible motive Stefano could have for wanting to meet the man she was sharing her life with. David stood smiling on the doorstep, looking casual and windswept, dressed in blue jeans, a matching denim shirt and a rather old tweed jacket with leather patches at the elbow. The scent of the pipe tobacco he sometimes smoked hung around him as he stepped forward to drop a light kiss on Cressida's mouth.

'Hello, love,' he said.

A cold voice rang out. 'Hadn't you better go and change, Cressida?' And there stood Stefano in the doorway, the thin smile on his mouth not echoed by the dark eyes.

'Hello,' said David interestedly, and Cressida saw Stefano's mouth curl in derision at the younger man's attitude.

It had been one of the things she had first admired about David—his easygoing nature, and his optimism. Even now, with an atmosphere which was as chilly as a winter's afternoon, with the forbidding stance of the handsome stranger who stood in her flat, and she, herself, clad in a short dressing-gown, it was plain to see that David was merely curious to know who Stefano was. And for some obscure reason, this irked her. If the situation had been reversed... She couldn't suppress a small shudder as she tried to imagine what Stefano's reaction would be if he had found her, only half dressed, with a strange man in her flat.

She stepped forward awkwardly to make the introductions. 'David Chalmers—this is Stefano di Camilla.'

David frowned, and, crossing his arms, he scratched the end of his nose in a thoughtful gesture. Cressida could see his mind working overtime.

'Di Camilla,' he said slowly. 'Haven't I heard—?'

'You may have heard my name being mentioned,' said Stefano smoothly, with scarcely a trace of the Italian accent which was so dominant when he was angry, or excited. 'I have the honour of providing some measure of support to the *superb* play of yours which Cressida is starring in.'

Hypocritical swine, thought Cressida, glaring at him, but meeting no answering response. How could he lay it on like that, after the nasty little asides he'd made about David's work?

David had stepped forward and grasped Stefano's hand eagerly. 'How do you do, Mr di Camilla?' he said eagerly. 'I'd heard Justin *mention* you, of course. We were getting worried—our other sponsors were threatening to pull out. You know, of course, how bad things are in this economic climate? I had no idea that events had progressed so far down the line. Justin might have *told* me,' he added, as an aggrieved afterthought.

'One of the conditions of my support was the need

for confidentiality until the deal was certain,' said Stefano blandly.

'Oh, of course, of course—I quite understand!' said David eagerly.

He was just like a bouncing little puppy, thought Cressida, trotting up to some wild creature eight times the size. Don't trust him an inch, she willed, wondering whether she would be strong enough to follow her own advice.

Stefano looked at the expensive timepiece on the strong wrist. 'It's getting late. I thought that perhaps the three of us could have supper together.'

David looked from him to Cressida, as if picking up the tension in the air for the first time. 'I don't think that Cressy feels up to it,' he said, a slightly nervous expression on his face.

'*Cressy*?' echoed Stefano, with soft incredulity, a mocking amusement twisting a corner of the firm lips.

She looked at him coldly. 'I like it,' she lied. 'It's less of a mouthful than Cressida.'

David stared at her in bewilderment. 'Is there something going on here that I should know about?'

Cressida sighed. How had she hoped to keep their past a secret, when they were already scrapping like the age-old combatants they really were?

Stefano smiled at the younger man. 'There is nothing "going on", David, other than the fact that I had already persuaded "Cressy" to go and put something pretty on, and let me take the two of you out to dinner—to celebrate my part in this exciting venture, yes?' His eyes crinkled in an easy smile which exuded charm, and she saw David automatically relax in response.

David smiled. 'That would be wonderful!' he enthused.

Cressida glowered at her husband. He had lost none of his manipulative skills, it seemed. He stared back at her, a cold gleam of mischief hiding in the dark eyes.

'Run along,' he said, in the manner of one talking to an imbecile. 'And put on your prettiest dress. David and I will wait here for you.'

It was not worth defying him; she knew that of old. Far better to humour him, and to find out exactly why he had made this unexpected reappearance in her life. She strode off to her bedroom, feeling his gaze lingering on her.

In her bedroom, she pulled off the satin wrap and threw it on the bed, feeling disgruntled and out of sorts. Her 'prettiest dress' indeed! If anything was less likely to make her choose a dress, then that was.

Deliberately, she pulled out some close-fitting white jeans and a soft white cotton roll-neck sweater. Flat white pumps completed the outfit, and as she brushed and plaited the thick hair and expertly applied the minimum amount of make-up she surveyed the result with satisfaction. She looked cool and modern—the antithesis of how Stefano had liked her to look. But when she returned, she was perplexed to see a look of satisfaction pass over the handsome olive features.

David, who seemed to be in the middle of explaining his ambition to one day own his own theatre, paused in mid-sentence as he looked up at Cressida. 'Oh, you're ready,' he said mildly, getting to his feet. 'Can I just use the bathroom?'

'Of course,' said Cressida reluctantly, for once

wishing that David had foisted an extravagant compliment on her, had put a possessive arm around her waist and told Stefano just where to go, instead of agreeing with everything he said.

When he had left the room, Stefano moved closer. 'You look very beautiful, *cara*,' he said huskily. 'Very beautiful.'

'Really?' she enquired. 'How very surprising that you should say so—because you didn't like me to wear trousers, did you? You hated me covering up my legs. Men wore trousers, not women—that was part of your ridiculous sexual stereotyping, wasn't it, Stefano?'

But it was not the expected irritation that she saw on his face, but a smile of triumph, as though he was playing a game with her—making up the rules, and one step ahead of her all the time.

'Which of course is why you wore them?' he suggested, a challenge lighting the dark eyes.

She inclined her head and shrugged. 'Not particularly,' she lied. 'What you do or don't consider to be suitable is really of no concern to me.' But to her fury he actually laughed.

'Oh, Cressida,' he murmured. 'No longer so docile. You have learnt to answer back.'

She turned away, the colour flaring in her cheeks. Answer back applying a little logic, as opposed to a highly emotional response, was what she presumed he meant. Perhaps if she had learnt to do that all that time ago. Perhaps if she had not been so intimidated by his family, his friends, him. Perhaps...

She walked over to the sideboard, and, with a hand which she defied to tremble, lifted a bottle of soda-water and tipped it into an empty glass. It was warm and it was flat, but it refreshed her dry mouth, and the action of drinking it allowed her time to re-gather her composure, so that by the time she had put the glass down and turned to face him, all trace of discomfiture had been carefully erased from her features, her cheeks their normal milky paleness, her green eyes calm.

The dark eyes had narrowed questioningly. 'You were miles away just now,' he said softly. 'Where?'

Her voice was steely, memories of wretched isolation within the marriage giving her strength. 'Remembering,' she told him. 'Our marriage. Reminding myself just how...' But the sound of a tap being turned off and David reappearing from the bathroom, his face wreathed in smiles, obviously anticipating his supper with relish, interrupted her.

As Cressida could have predicted, the evening was an unqualified disaster, starting with the car journey to the restaurant. David, being a keen environmentalist, had caught the bus, and therefore needed a lift. The three of them went outside to Stefano's car, which was a sleek black model with an excuse for a back seat.

'How ridiculous,' said Cressida waspishly. 'A midget couldn't fit into that.'

'It's designed as a two-seater,' said Stefano smoothly. 'David will have to curl his legs up.'

'*I'll* go in the back,' said Cressida.

'You will not. David is the man, is he not?'

His voice seemed to express some doubt, thought Cressida furiously as she slammed the door shut. She must have been *mad* to submit to this. The deal was that the three of them have supper, and she hoped to

goodness that Stefano would not spend the entire meal
baiting David, because, when it came to one-
upmanship, David was just not in the same league as
Stefano.

But within two minutes of being seated at one of
the best tables in the discreet Italian restaurant Stefano
had chosen, she realised that he was far too clever to
display open animosity towards her date. Conversely,
he showed nothing but interest in David's work, his
mouth betraying nothing more than the merest quirk
of amusement when the playwright began to wax lyr-
ical about one of his political heroes. To her chagrin,
she found herself comparing the two men, wondering
why traits of David's character which she'd once
found so enchantingly different should now irritate her
when stood next to Stefano's cool brand of charm. For
charm he most certainly had. He could still have the
eye of every woman in the restaurant turned rapa-
ciously in his direction, and the smiling ear of every
waiter in the place.

'What will you have, Cressida?' he enquired urbanely. 'Or would you like me to order for you?'

'No, thank you,' she answered sweetly, and turned
to the waiter and ordered her meal in halting Italian,
bringing a look of almost startled surprise to Stefano's
face, which puzzled her.

'I didn't know you could speak Italian!' said David
with admiration.

'I can't, really,' she said shakily. She had nearly
given herself away. 'Just a smattering.' She could not
meet Stefano's eyes. She had tried to learn it, for him.
She had thought that the shared language might bring
them closer—might bridge the chasm which separated

her from the rest of his life—so she had battled with her textbooks, praying that it, something, anything might save their ailing marriage. But of course, it hadn't. She had first tried it out while shopping during their regular weekend trips to Italy, but the shop assistants in the nearby town, puzzled by Signor di Camilla's wife attempting to shop for vegetables instead of dispatching one of the servants to do it, had deliberately failed to understand her. She remembered how abruptly Stefano had made them leave dinner parties, presumably because he was acutely embarrassed by her faltering attempts to conquer the strange new language. And after a few months of this she had given up—reverting to her native tongue, slipping back into her curious role of outsider.

'Some wine?' Stefano urged, bringing her back to the present with a start.

She nodded, half imagining that she had seen a flash of comprehension in the velvet brown eyes, but they were hooded immediately by the thickly lashed lids. She gulped a mouthful of the rich red wine—grateful enough for the almost instant warmth it sent flooding through her veins, but then regretting that she hadn't declined, that she hadn't left her senses crystal-clear. For after finishing the glass, a torpid sense of warmth enveloped her, and she found that her brain simply wouldn't function with any degree of logic, because why else should she find that she could only tear her eyes away with difficulty from the handsome dark-eyed man who sat before her? He was talking exclusively to David, as though he had totally forgotten her presence, and, illogically—just as his earlier and suggestive attentions in the flat had infuriated her—now she was just as irritated by his seeming disregard.

Throwing caution to the wind, she rashly let the waiter pour her some more of the rich wine, and as she sipped she looked from underneath her lashes, observing him surreptitiously. She found her eyes travelling from the strong profile, the jutting jaw, and the firm column of his neck, down to where the fine material of his shirt clung to the solid muscle of his chest. When they were first married she would have sat in a similar restaurant, just revelling in the sheer beauty of him, scarcely able to believe that this gorgeous man was really her husband. But how differently the evening would have ended, with them standing face to face in their London flat, exchanging little kisses, before the desire overcame them, and fine garments would be shrugged off with apparent disregard in their eagerness to lie naked together.

Stefano was looking at her, his eyes intent. 'Your eyes are very heavy, Cressida. You are, I think, very tired?'

She bit her lip, praying that he should not be able to guess what had been going on in her mind, that she had been mad enough to remember their lovemaking. What was she trying to do to herself? The whole evening was a farce. It *was* ridiculous to think that she could dine amicably with the man she had once loved body and soul—to act as though the bonds which had tied them were no more. The longer she sat with him, the more difficult it was to convince herself that what she had done had been the right thing to do—the only thing to do.

She nodded. 'Yes,' she agreed. 'I'm very tired.'

Stefano paid the bill, and as he helped her on with her light jacket his hands brushed against her shoulders. It was the lightest of touches, but the physical contact was like a body-blow—as far removed from the chaste hugs which David occasionally bestowed on her as it was possible to be.

And she was surprised to discover that Stefano planned to drop her off first, driving David home afterwards. Had she perhaps thought that he would make a pass at her again—to demonstrate the considerable power of his sexuality? Was that it?

Well, he hadn't touched her. And as she made her way wearily to the bathroom to brush her teeth, she wondered quite why the overriding emotion she should be experiencing that he had not was one of something that closely resembled disappointment, rather than relief.

CHAPTER FOUR

AFTER a restless night, fraught with imaginings about Stefano's intentions, Cressida rose pale and dark-eyed. Some time in the early hours, she had lain wide awake, tossing and turning while her mind tried to cope with imagining what the reality of having Stefano as her play's main backer would mean.

Would he use his power for his own aims—whatever they might be? She was still no clearer about what lay behind his new foray into the arts. He had hinted at profit, but reflection during the long hours of the night had convinced her that this could not possibly be his sole motivation. A mould-breaking play by a relatively unknown playwright—these were not the hallmarks of a deal which would attract a man as rich and as powerful as Stefano. Which left her mind buzzing with the disconcerting thought that it must be *her* presence which had brought him here. But why? They had parted bitterly, with acrimony on both sides, and accusations flying. Wounding words which had left deep scars. So why was he here?

Cressida looked at the clock on her bedside table. It was still early—just after eight. Time enough for her to decide just what was she going to do. Surely not sit back and allow Stefano to haunt her, to hover on the outskirts of her life like a threatening shadow?

She was no longer an innocent of nineteen, cowed by his experience of the world. And one thing she *had* learned from her broken marriage was that a problem left to fester was far worse than confronting it from the outset. She was not going to fade away anxiously trying to surmise just what he was doing—damn the man, she would go directly to him, and ask him.

She showered and dressed quickly, dressing casually in the faded blue jeans she normally wore for rehearsal, with a baggy cotton shirt tucked into them, and her hair tied back into a thick but neat French plait. Eschewing make-up, she made herself some coffee and sat back to wait for nine o'clock.

She didn't need to check the number—it was engraved on her memory. The di Camilla family had outlets in all the major cities. When she had met Stefano, he had been over in England to boost the fortunes of the London office. She hadn't believed that it was possible for anyone to work quite as hard as Stefano had done. During their marriage, they spent weekdays in London, where she scarcely saw him. He was so busy at the office, and at night all he wanted to do was to make love to her and fall into bed into an exhausted sleep. And weekends were spent at the villa outside Rome, where she had felt as cosseted and as lonely as a bird in a gilded cage... Cressida frowned as the hands of her watch moved inexorably towards office-opening time. She was nervous about contacting him—though heaven only knew why she should be. Surely she had a *right* to know just why he was back, and besides, there was the little matter of divorce to discuss... He had ignored her solicitor's letter, but he damned well couldn't ignore her.

As she lifted the receiver and began to dial the number, she noticed that her hand was shaking slightly, and she hesitated. Why bother phoning first? Wasn't forewarned forearmed? Why not take a cab directly to the di Camilla headquarters, and confront him?

She got to her feet, donned a loose navy duffel coat, and sped outside before she could change her mind. She had to wait at least ten minutes before a cab appeared. Life, she reflected wryly, was nothing like the plays or occasional film she'd worked in—in those, taxis appeared like magic!

But by the time she reached the towering glass and chrome structure of the di Camilla building, her resolve had threatened to leave her, and it took a huge, gulping breath of air before her pulse steadied to a near-normal rate. It had been ages since she'd ventured near here. She'd deliberately stayed away from this part of the city, terrified that she might come into contact with Stefano, or a member of his family. For in those early days, hadn't she desperately veered between knowing that she had done the best thing by leaving him and a crazy, destructive urge to run back to him?

As she pushed the glass door open, she reflected that it was also a long time since she'd been within these marble portals, and the sense of wonder at the sheer lavishness of the interior which she'd felt on her first visit returned to make her steps falter very slightly—momentarily making her become again the innocent young redhead who had come here to meet Stefano for lunch. Another deep breath, and then she flashed a bright, professional smile at the glacial blonde beauty who sat behind the desk, wondering what right she had to resent her beauty. Stefano had always employed beautiful women. Beautiful *and* bright—he used to demand the best, and he always got it.

'May I help you?' the beauty asked, her cool voice expressing some doubt, the faintest familiar twang to her voice making Cressida's heart sink to her boots. She was Italian. In the pockets of her old duffel coat, her fists clenched. What if…what if this woman had been brought over by Stefano? She mustn't be naïve— it had been over two years since she had left him and he would have had lots of women in that time, a man with his particular appetites. Was she really ready to be exposed to any evidence of that?

The beauty gave a scarcely audible sigh. 'May I help you?' she repeated.

Cressida took a deep breath. 'Yes. I'd like to speak with Mr di Camilla, please.'

Dark eyes widened. The look said it all, as it travelled from the pale, unmade-up face, down the faded duffel coat, to rest on the ubiquitous denims.

She smiled—not an unkind smile, thought Cressida. More an apologetic one.

'Signor *Stefano* di Camilla?' the girl verified.

'Yes, please.' The girl's poorly disguised incredulity was only adding to Cressida's feeling of discomfort, but she was determined to stand her ground. She had come here to see Stefano, and see him she would. And she was not going to be cowed by his receptionist, or let her see just how uncomfortable she felt. 'Perhaps you'd care to ring through to his office?' she suggested calmly. 'I'm sure he will see me.'

The girl gave a slight shake of the head, and raised

two beautifully manicured hands briefly in the air, in such an extravagantly un-English gesture, so reminiscent of her husband, that Cressida had to close her eyes briefly against the unexpectedly sharp pain in her breast. When she opened them again, the girl was watching her warily.

'I am sorry,' she said. 'But Signor di Camilla will see no one without appointment.' She smiled and lowered her sleek blonde head to begin to write in a file, in a politely emphatic dismissal.

'He will see *me*!' Cressida's trained voice rang out around the vast foyer, and the girl looked startled. Her gaze went automatically to Cressida's torso, frowning a little as she did so, as if she could hope to see through the material of the coat, and Cressida felt physically sick. Did she think that she was some slighted lover, turning up pregnant and desperate, demanding to be seen by him? She leaned forward. 'I want to see him now,' she demanded urgently.

The girl shrank back in alarm, her hand going to beneath the desk, presumably, thought Cressida, to summon help, but before she could do so there was some slight movement, and both women's eyes were drawn to the foot of the stairs, where a dark figure stood, watching.

The girl behind the desk sprang to her feet. '*Signore!*' she exclaimed. 'I was just explaining…'

He didn't appear to hear her; his hooded eyes were fixed intently on Cressida. She stared back at him, struck by how sleek, how dark, and how powerful he looked, in his pale grey suit, even more at ease than usual, here in his own environment.

His face was impossible to read—the strong dark

features set in an implacable mask—and yet the blood
began to thunder and roar in her ears as her pulse-rate
rose.

She supposed she must be like one of those dogs—
Pavlov's dogs—conditioned to salivate whenever a
bell was rung. She was really no different—her body
instinctively reacted to Stefano, her senses clamoured
to life in his presence. But that was nothing more than
a conditioned response to him.

She felt her speeding pulses slow just a little. 'I
want to talk to you,' she said, hearing the unmistakable
intake of breath from the receptionist, and the implied
disapproval behind the sound gave her a heady rush
of adrenalin as she stared firmly into the cold, dark
eyes.

'Shall I call Security?' asked the receptionist nervously.

Stefano laughed, white teeth gleaming like a cat
about to pounce. 'Security? No, indeed. I need no protection against my wife. Not yet, anyway,' he murmured, his eyes glinting in acknowledgement of her
fiery expression. 'Perhaps we can have them on stand-
by?' he mocked.

'Your *wife*?' The question was incredulous, and, bizarrely, it filled Cressida with fury. She turned her
heavy-lashed green eyes haughtily on the girl.

'Yes, his wife,' she said coolly. 'You seem surprised?'

Stefano had moved closer. He stood a few feet
away, and, seeing the pristine whiteness of his im-
maculately pressed silk shirt, she found herself wondering, jealously, who was responsible for its appearance. 'Let us continue this discussion somewhere a

little quieter,' he said in a silky voice which did little to disguise his steely intent, his hand taking her by the forearm in a deceptively soft movement, and she drew back at the contact, her pupils dilating underneath the glare of the foyer lights as she felt his touch. Words deserted her as he led her towards a lift in the far corner of the foyer.

'I do not wish to be disturbed,' he called over his shoulder in a voice curiously devoid of emotion, but as soon as the door of the lift had slid shut behind them he turned to her, his eyes travelling over her, his eyebrows lifting to question.

'So tell me, did you enjoy making your little scene?' he queried.

Still smarting from the blonde receptionist's cursory dismissal, Cressida glared at him. 'You should tell your beautiful custodian not to be so damned uppity in future.'

'So you think she's beautiful, do you?' he mused. 'Yes, I have to agree with you. She is. Very.'

Quite how she stopped herself from raking her fingernails down the side of that smooth olive face, Cressida didn't quite know, but the madness within her died almost instantly as she reminded herself that it was nothing to do with her if he was involved with another woman. *Nothing at all.* 'I found her manner rude,' she said.

'Oh?' He seemed to be expecting some clarification.

'She wasn't going to let me see you.' She glared.

He shrugged. 'Why should she?'

'Because I'm your *wife*!'

His voice was cold. 'But not for very much longer, so I believe?'

It was as if he had punched her in the solar plexus—yes, she had asked him for a divorce, but his first acknowledgment that the marriage really *was* over hit her like a body-blow. All the fight and her breath went out of her, and she stared at him, white-faced, biting her lip to stop it trembling.

His eyes narrowed at her reaction and he laid a hand on her rigid forearm. 'Come,' he said, in a gentler tone, which set off a silent scream of yearning in her head. 'The lift is no place to talk. Let us continue this discussion in my office.'

He pushed a button, and the door slid open and she allowed him to lead her stiffly across a vast carpeted area, past a secretary, who spoke quickly to him in Italian, but he shook his head. '*Adesso no!*' he shot out tersely.

Still dazed from his last remark, it took several seconds for her surroundings to register, and when they did she saw that his office had altered dramatically. Once, it had been dark, with a great deal of old wood, old paintings, subtle rugs of great value—but all these had now been swept away to be replaced by lighter, more modern fittings. To Cressida, who had disliked the older-style, antique-filled version, it was a vast improvement, but it unsettled her. How much else of his life was different? she wondered, before quickly reminding herself again that his life was nothing to do with her any more.

'Sit down.' His tanned hand indicated a small sofa which sat against one of the walls. 'I'll ring for some coffee—you look as if you could do with some. Anyone would think you hadn't slept.'

Oh, why had she dashed straight over here without

covering up the evidence of her poor night? Now his insufferable ego would be fed with the satisfying thought that she was losing sleep over him. 'I don't want to sit down! And I don't want any of your wretched coffee!'

He ignored her and bent down to speak into an intercom. 'Well, I do.' There was an answering click, and he smiled, speaking rapidly in Italian.

Cressida was forced to sit there, fuming, while another elegant young woman carried in a tray of steaming and fragrant coffee, her glance stealing curiously over at Cressida.

Stefano poured himself some coffee. 'Are you sure you won't change your mind?' he queried, as he added a heaped spoonful of sugar to his cup. 'It's espresso—your favourite.'

And the smell *was* ridiculously tantalising, but for some reason this confident assumption infuriated her. 'It is *not* my favourite coffee, Stefano. Not any more. I've changed.'

Dark eyes narrowed. 'Indeed? And how have you changed, *cara*?'

The indulgent way in which he spoke would have provoked a chilly smile and a shrug if it had been spoken by anyone else, but Stefano had always had the knack of making her open her mouth before she had engaged her brain. 'I'm my own woman now,' she asserted.

He grimaced. 'There speaks the true feminist, hmm?'

Flames danced before her eyes. 'If that's how you like to see it. Unlike you, I happen to believe in equality.'

'You do me a disservice,' he said, grim-faced. 'Either that, or you have a defectively poor memory. You seem to forget that I allowed you to continue with your career.'

His choice of words fuelled her slowly erupting anger. 'Allowed?' she exclaimed incredulously. '*Allowed*? How very good of you, Stefano. And, yes, you allowed me to work—but only so long as it suited *you*. The moment that my work in any way interfered with your life was the moment you delivered your ultimatum.'

The dark eyes had narrowed to impenetrable slits. 'We obviously had different expectations within the marriage,' he said tightly. 'I did not expect my wife to be working in one country while I worked in another—'

'But it wasn't like that!' she interrupted hotly. The work became my only salvation, she wanted to say, but Stefano wouldn't understand that in a million years. He had never listened in the past, so why on earth should he listen now? She shook her head sadly. 'Oh, what's the use? Just tell me why you decided to back David's play,' she asked, her voice tremulous with emotion.

He looked at her assessingly. 'Why do you think?'

'No more games, please, Stefano. A straight answer to a straight question.'

A half-smile lifted the corners of the coldly beautiful mouth as he shrugged his broad shoulders.

'One of my contacts told me that you were appearing in this—how do you say?—''fringe'' production. Perhaps it amuses me to watch you perform.'

Did he see a look cross her face, some naïve kind

of eagerness which she couldn't suppress? Was that what prompted his next slamming response?

'Oh, don't make too much of it, *cara*—your play is only one of a *number* of arts projects I'm involved in. We have decided to diversify into the arts.'

'Have you?' she asked flatly.

'Mmm. We have.' The dark eyes narrowed. 'But naturally, there is another reason for my interest in your current activities. Why, I wonder, is my wife so eager to get a divorce? Is there someone else in her life? Someone she hopes to marry?'

If only he knew how far he had strayed from the truth. 'I'm glad that you've brought up the subject of divorce, Stefano.'

'Oh? And why is that?'

'We both know it's over, Stefano.' The words came out in an unsteady rush. 'We've been separated for over two years now and legally there's nothing stopping us and...' Her voice faltered.

'And?' he prompted, his head resting back in his hands as he surveyed her without emotion.

'I'd like a divorce as soon as possible—please.' The automatically polite entreaty tacked on to the end of the stilted request made the hard line of his mouth twist in derision, and she found herself having to speak again, in fear that if she didn't she might do something she would always regret. Like cry. 'There's nothing to stop us,' she finished hollowly.

'And what if I don't want a divorce?' he said slowly, the intense gleam of the narrowed eyes holding her firmly in its light.

Hope stirred within her like a foolish flame. 'Not

want a divorce?' she repeated stupidly. 'Why on earth should you not want one?'

He shrugged and stretched his long legs comfortably out in front of him. She saw the grey folds of his trousers fall to emphasise the powerful thrust of his thighs.

'Perhaps it suits me to stay married,' he murmured.

'Suits you? What do you mean?'

A slow smile spread over his face. He made an upward little movement with his hands. 'You know how it is, Cressida. A divorced man is at a certain disadvantage, mmm?'

She stared at him uncomprehendingly.

'Whereas,' he continued, 'a man who is separated is—shall we say?—*safe* from the intentions of women whose sole purpose in life is to settle down.' He smiled. 'Now do you understand?'

Bile rose in her stomach. She stood up, gripping the arm of the sofa as she did so. 'Are you trying to tell me that you won't give me a divorce because that would make you easy prey for husband hunters?' she demanded.

A wry half-smile lifted the corners of his mouth. 'I am saying that it is a consideration,' he conceded.

They told you to count to ten in times of severe stress, thought Cressida bizarrely—well, she doubted whether slowly counting to a thousand could do anything to dispel the painful, murderous rage which his words had evoked. And wouldn't he just love to know it? She could just imagine his satisfied smile if she hurled herself beating and kicking and scratching like a hell-cat at him.

She was grateful at that moment for her dramatic

training, because when she met his eyes again her face was as composed as his. She even managed the polite kind of half-smile she would use to greet some casual acquaintance. She had accomplished nothing by coming here—but, if she had thought it through rationally, had she ever really expected to? And had she ever been able to resort to rationale where Stefano was concerned?

'There's no point in talking to you,' she said coolly. 'You'll be hearing from my solicitor.'

'Of course,' he said urbanely, equally cool.

She managed to walk to the door when all she wanted to do was run, feeling his silent, assessing gaze at her back, wishing that she could walk out of this room and never set eyes on him again.

And as she turned the door-handle, he spoke.

'*Cara.*' The softness of his tone lulled her, making it impossible for her to disregard it, impossible not to turn round. Hoping…hoping for what? That he had changed his mind about not giving her a divorce?

She turned. 'Yes?'

'*Ciao*,' he murmured mockingly, and somehow the casual Italian farewell brought it all back in a blinding rush—the day he had watched her leave him. But it had not been '*ciao*' that he had said then. She would remember his flat, cold 'goodbye' for as long as she lived.

'Go to hell,' she said, knowing that she had to get out of here, away from him.

Hoping for his agreement to a divorce? she had wondered. No, that hadn't been what she'd been hoping for.

Not at all.

CHAPTER FIVE

CRESSIDA managed to compose herself enough to walk coolly past the curious eyes of the blonde in Reception, pushing open the gleaming doors of the building before stepping outside to drink in a huge gulp of air, as if it would revive her. Sweat lay in fine beads on her upper lip and brow, and she half considered removing her duffel coat before she took in that the day was chilly and the air filled with a light drizzle and that in a minute she would cool down and calm down, just as soon as the effect of her conversation with Stefano wore off. But nevertheless, she stood there for several seconds, disorientated, until her steps automatically took her towards the Tube.

Only when she was buying her ticket did she finally come to her senses, realising that it was ten-thirty and that rehearsals were due to start in half an hour.

Rehearsals. How the hell could she get through a rehearsal, feeling the way she did, when all she really wanted to do was to go back to the safe haven of her flat and lie on her narrow bed, howling until there were no tears left? Which of course was out of the question. She was a professional, and professionals simply did not behave in that way. Once, like yesterday, was enough.

As she stepped on to the grey and smoke-grimed

platform, Cressida wished, not for the first time in her life, that she had some nice, normal, *ordinary* career, with normal hours and normal expectations. Where you weren't expected to pin a smile on your face and become someone else when sometimes you weren't even sure who you were yourself...

She folded her ticket obsessively into tiny squares. She was as mixed up as ever about Stefano. Nothing was as black and white as she'd convinced herself it was in that two years apart. Why else would she feel so churned up and confused when she saw him?

As the train thundered through an inky tunnel, she closed her eyes.

She was badly in need of someone to talk to, someone to help her make sense of the confusion of thoughts which were rushing around her head. But to confide in anyone connected with the play was out of the question, and she certainly didn't feel she could tell David.

And she had surprisingly few friends—the life of an actress was perfect if you needed an excuse for not starting up a relationship. Periods of unemployment followed by spells of working in vastly different jobs—both combined to allow actors to pursue a fairly nomadic life, if that was what they wanted. And that had certainly been what Cressida had wanted. She'd let no one close to her.

Except for Judy, her flatmate and confidante in those early days of drama school, before Stefano had made her exclusively his.

Judy would understand. Judy had been there at the beginning—surely she would remember the rollercoaster of emotions which Stefano had always provoked in her?

In the brightly lit street to the theatre, Cressida fumbled around for some loose change, and telephoned Judy at work.

After initial greetings, she got to the point. 'I wondered if you'd have lunch with me?'

'Sure,' Judy replied. 'Love to. When?'

'I know it's short notice, but—how about today?'

There was the shortest of pauses at the other end, then the sound of paper being rustled. 'Let me see... Yup, that's fine, Cressida. Name your time and place.'

They arranged to meet at the theatre at two, and in the meantime Cressida attempted to put her heart and soul into the rehearsal and banish that final memory of Stefano looking deep into her eyes as she had left his office. If you want to remember anything, then remember why he won't give you a divorce, she reminded herself bitterly—so that he can conduct his dalliances without fear of becoming ensnared in marriage.

She gave the best performance she could, but was glad nevertheless when they broke for lunch. She spent five minutes in the washroom, brushing her hair and rubbing her fists into her cheeks to bring some colour back into them, before hurrying to the rehearsal room to meet Judy.

She found her joking with other members of the cast, most of whom she knew, who were variously rolling on the floor and tickling a rumbustious toddler who was running rings around them.

Judy looked up as she saw Cressida enter and gave her a wide grin. 'Hiya, hon!' Then, reverting to a

phrase which was so typical of her, exclaimed, 'My
God! But you're pale, pale, pale!'

So her efforts at camouflage had been in vain,
thought Cressida ruefully. 'Hi!' she smiled. 'Hi, Jack!'
And she picked the small boy up and swung him round
to delighted screams.

'You didn't tell us Judy was coming!' said Jenna.
'We thought we could all go out for lunch round the
corner.'

Judy stood up as Cressida shot her an agonised look.
'I don't think so,' she said firmly. 'I think this is just
the two—or should I say three—of us. And anyway—
no one in their right mind would want to eat with my
son out of choice!'

There were exaggerated groans all round as Judy
scooped Jack out of Cressida's arms. 'Lead on,
Macduff!' she misquoted jokingly.

They found a nearby café where they ordered sandwiches and coffee and Jack sat contentedly munching
from a bag of crisps.

'He's so good,' observed Cressida, as her godson
pushed a potato chip into her chin.

'He's adaptable,' said Judy, trying but not managing
to conceal her pride. 'With a working mum, he needs
to be. Right!' she said briskly. 'That's the pleasantries
dealt with. What's wrong?'

Cressida looked up at her. 'Is it that obvious?' she
asked.

'Yup. To me, anyway. You're jumpy. You're pale.
You're unhappy.'

The waitress brought their sandwiches, but Cressida
pushed her plate away. 'It's Stefano,' she said bluntly.

Judy froze stock-still in the middle of handing Jack

his beaker of milk. 'Stefano?' she queried. 'What about him?'

'He's back.'

'What do you mean, he's *back*? Back where?'

'Back here. In London.'

'So? The family have always had business here, haven't they? You don't have to see him.'

Cressida drummed her long fingers nervously on the Formica table. 'You don't understand. I *do* have to see him. He's our new angel—he's backing the play.'

'*Whaaa-t*?' Judy spoke so loudly and so incredulously that Jack dropped his beaker.

'It's true,' sighed Cressida, retrieving the vessel and handing it back to him. 'He's back in my life—and how.' But, close as they might be, nothing would prompt her to tell Judy of their first encounter in her dressing-room. How could she possibly admit to the humiliating weakness which came over her whenever he was around? Look at the way she'd been with him, moving with frustrated need beneath his hands, opening up underneath his touch like a parched flower in a storm. She shook her head despairingly.

Judy was frowning at her. 'Just why has Stefano started financing plays? He hates the theatre.'

'I don't *know*,' replied Cressida desperately. 'And as far as I know it's not any other plays—it's this one. It's because…because…'

'Because you're in it,' said Judy slowly.

'Yes. *Yes*.' Cressida stared at her friend. 'But how did you know?'

'Oh, come on—credit me with a little more intelligence than that. You wouldn't need to be Einstein to see the connection. It's obvious—what I'd like to know is why?'

Cressida's eyelids sank over the huge green eyes. Why indeed? 'Who could ever tell what was going on in that steel trap of a mind?' she said bitterly. 'You know Stefano.'

But Judy shook her head. 'No, I don't, Cressida,' she said frankly. 'I met him lots of times before you were married, but I never really knew him. Not the way you did.'

'I don't know if I ever really knew him either,' whispered Cressida. For hadn't he always held something of himself back? The apparent closeness of the early days had swiftly been eroded by the day-to-day living of their married life, and at the end of those eighteen months of marriage she had felt that she knew little more of Stefano than when they'd first met.

'Has he said anything about the divorce?'

'Only that he hasn't decided whether or not to give me one.'

'*Whaa-t?*' exclaimed Judy, for the second time. 'Why the hell not?'

This too was humiliating. 'Because...' stumbled Cressida, her voice sounding dangerously close to breaking. 'Because being single again might expose him to women intent on marriage. But being separated apparently provides some kind of protection.'

'Bastard!' said Judy, with feeling.

Cressida took a mouthful of coffee. 'The question is—what am I going to *do*?'

'There's not a lot you can do,' said Judy practically. 'You can't leave the play now and let the company down, and even if you did—that would be like letting him win. And it's only a limited run, isn't it?'

'Eight weeks.'

'Well, then—just do the run, then you'll be rid of him. And don't let him frighten you over the divorce—if he won't let you have it on the grounds of two years' separation then you'll just have to wait the five. There's no one else you're keen to settle down with, is there? What about this David guy you brought to see us? Is that serious?'

'Heavens, no!' denied Cressida, with a vehemence which startled them both, and under Judy's perceptive gaze she dropped her eyelids, a slow flush of colour painting itself over her high cheekbones. 'Cressida,' said Judy softly, 'look at me.'

Reluctantly, Cressida raised her shadowed green eyes. 'What?' she whispered.

'What aren't you telling me?'

She shook her head. 'Nothing.'

Judy sighed. 'All right. I don't want to pry if you don't want me to—but tell me something. How do you feel about Stefano now, after all this time?'

Cressida returned her friend's gaze helplessly. How did she feel? There wasn't a word in the English language which could be used to describe the dizzying and betraying emotions which had assailed her since his return. She'd known fear, disbelief, desire, hatred, sadness and—what else?

Judy was staring at her, her eyes wide with incredulity. 'My God,' she said disbelievingly. 'I don't believe it! You're still in love with him, aren't you? After all he's done to you—you're still in love with him!'

'No, of course I'm not,' replied Cressida, wondering why, even with all the ringing conviction with which she spoke them, the words should sound, even to her own ears, hollow and untrue.

CHAPTER SIX

THE next day started badly. Cressida, who'd had a miserable night, finally dozed off just after dawn and consequently overslept. The traffic to the theatre was horrendous, and she only just had enough money in her purse to pay for the cab. As she fumbled around for some loose change, it occurred to her that sooner or later she was going to have to come back down to earth. Just because she had seen Stefano again didn't mean that she should try and emulate his kind of lifestyle. She had given all that up when she had left him. Taxis, in case she was still labouring under a misapprehension, were *out*—it was back to buses as far as she was concerned.

'I'm sorry I can't give you a tip.' She gave the driver an apologetic smile.

'Don't mention it. Have a nice day,' he said sarcastically, and swerved off at speed through a puddle, splashing Cressida's jeans with icy cold and filthy water.

'Thanks,' she called at the disappearing tail-lights, her mouth curving a little in wry observation as she noted that the taxi driver had not fallen victim to her smile. And who could blame him? She looked an absolute wreck, no more and no less. Perhaps lack of sleep was something she was just going to have to get used to, pacing the floor or going over her lines in the middle of the night in an attempt to push the constant thoughts of Stefano from her mind. She'd covered up the shadows beneath her eyes with foundation, but the dark blue drifts were there for all but the least discerning to see.

Early this morning she had made a decision, and it was a decision she meant to keep. She was going to put Stefano right out of her mind. Completely, she thought, as she stood watching the retreating taxi.

But this was obviously going to be easier said than done, since when she arrived at the rehearsal room she discovered that Stefano was the chief topic of conversation, and that every member of the company seemed determined to talk about him. Apparently he had taken Justin and Alexia out for dinner the previous week to celebrate becoming the play's new backer. Cressida walked into the rehearsal room to find that Alexia had a captive audience as she described the evening.

'I wasn't allowed to say anything before,' she babbled. 'It was all so *secret*.'

'Where did he take you?' asked Jenna.

Alexia pursed her lips into an over-the-top pout which made Cressida privately think that she had gone into the wrong profession—she should have been a kissogram girl!

'The Scala,' she announced. 'The best Italian restaurant in the country. I was told it was impossible to get a booking there.' She sighed. 'But *he* managed it— *and* it was last-minute.'

'What was it like?' queried the costume mistress.

'What?' smiled Alexia secretly.

'The food, you idiot!' laughed Lydia. 'Everyone says the food is superb.'

Alexia's china-blue eyes widened like a child's. 'Oh, the food!' she scoffed. 'Believe me—even if I'd been starving I wouldn't have looked at the food with a man like Stefano sitting opposite me. Every woman in the place could hardly keep their eyes off him. Even the waitress looked as though she'd like to eat him up. I tell you,' she smiled artlessly, 'I felt exactly the same as that waitress!'

There were loud guffaws of laughter, and Cressida pinned a determined smile on her lips, furious with herself for caring what Alexia did with Stefano, resolutely pushing out the pictures of Alexia's blue eyes darkening with pleasure as he bent to kiss her.

Cressida waited for the rehearsal to begin and wished she'd brought a sweater—the rehearsal room was *freezing*. David was there, she noted, as she hung up her duffel coat and dabbed ineffectually at the water splashes on her jeans. He appeared to be in a hurry, giving her only the briefest of waves before going into a huddle with Justin. She sighed. All his earlier eagerness to talk to her at any opportunity seemed to have deserted him—she supposed that she had the other night's *ménage à trois* to thank for that, and wondered just what Stefano had said to him in the car on the way home.

'We won't start yet,' said Justin. 'Take five—and grab a coffee.'

The company gladly obliged. Cressida perched on a stool next to Adrian, sipping strong black coffee thankfully.

'You better now?' asked Adrian conversationally.

'Better?'

He raised his eyes heavenwards. 'Short memory, darling,' he teased. 'Don't tell me you've forgotten your dramatic collapse at rehearsal the other day.' He started intoning in the manner of a newsreader. 'Beautiful red-haired actress Cressida Carter was today recovering from a mysterious faint on stage at the Carlisle Theatre. When asked what had caused the attack, she was heard to simper—' his accent changed to deep south American '—"Honey—when I saw that *man* I just went out like a light!"'

Cressida coloured.

'What man?' asked Jenna, eager for gossip.

'You remember.' Adrian's eyes glinted mischievously in Cressida's direction. 'Our dark-haired angel. The mysterious Signor di Camilla. Seen by the lovely Alexia leaving our leading lady's dressing-room. Rumour has it that her lipstick was smudged, and her mascara smeared.' He placed his fists on either hip. 'My dears!' he exclaimed. 'I think Cressida must be in *lurve!*'

'Oh, shut up,' said Cressida, attempting to inject a note of humour into her voice, knowing that the only way to prevent gossip in the close world of the theatre was to make light of it. 'He's more Alexia's type. Besides, I've got David.'

Adrian began whistling innocently, but then Justin stood up to start the rehearsal, which thankfully, thought Cressida, put an end to any more speculation.

Justin's first words quickly put paid to her hopes of a quiet day.

'Script change, folks,' he announced. 'Alexia's made the necessary alterations.'

New scripts were handed out, and they studied them. Cressida frowned slightly as she perused her copy. The play's setting had been changed. Originally set in the South of France, the first act had been moved to a flat in Paris. She looked at Justin in bemusement.

'But all my costumes will have to change,' she pointed out.

'I know.' Justin nodded. 'Stella says there's no problem with that.'

Adrian waved the new script in the air. 'Forgive me saying this, but we've now got Cressida and me wearing "light summer wardrobe", whereas before we were in swimsuits.'

'So?' Justin crunched one of his peppermints aggressively.

'Oh, come on!' said Adrian. 'Let's not be naïve, Jus. Theatre-goers like—shall we say?—decorative scenery, and we'll be denying them that if we cover up Cressida's legs!'

'Now wait a minute,' started Cressida. 'There's no need to make me out to be some sort of bimbo.'

'Darling,' soothed Adrian, 'you got the part because of your superb talent—your looks are just incidental.'

She stared at Justin mulishly. 'Are you happy with these changes?'

He nodded, pushing his glasses further up his nose to indicate that the discussion was at an end. 'Sure, I'm happy. Now, can we *please* begin? I've got a play to get on by next week, and our new backer wants some sign of a return on his money.'

Cressida looked questioningly at David, but he was miles away, his head bent over his script, and she suddenly knew who was behind the sudden changes. Who else but Stefano? What had he objected to when he had visited that very first day when she'd passed out at the sight of him? 'Voyeurs' looking at her body, implying that she was being provocative by wearing the swimsuit. And, being Stefano, he wouldn't have simply disapproved in silence. Oh, no, somehow, like the low-down, manipulative snake he was, he had managed to get the whole first act rewritten. It was unbelievable!

She pushed her hand back through the thick red hair. Didn't he even care? Didn't it matter to him that it was *his* investment, and that by altering the play to suit his chauvinism he was compromising the artistic integrity? Integrity? She shut her wide mouth into a tight line. There was that word again. The word she doubted Stefano had ever heard of.

The rehearsal was dreadful. Tempers were frayed, not least the director's, and Adrian was obviously out-of-sorts, too. Cressida tried her best, but the new lines didn't seem to flow so well and her gestures felt wooden and unconvincing, and it was hard to put her anger out of her mind.

By lunchtime, she was gibbering with rage as she made her way to her dressing-room. One thing was for sure—he should not be allowed to get away with this kind of blatant interference, and she would damn well tell him. Or, better still—why not complain to Justin? Putting the personal element aside—wouldn't that be eminently more sensible? Because Justin would surely see that the changes were detrimental to the play itself.

On an impulse, she rushed off to ask Alexia where she could find Justin.

'He's in there.' Alexia jerked her head in the direction of one of the small offices along the corridor. 'But—'

But Cressida didn't stop to listen. Before she had time to change her mind, she rapped on the door, and pushed it open.

Justin sat at a desk, but he was not alone, for sitting beside him was the muscular frame of her husband, long legs encased in pale linen, crossed arrogantly at ease, his eyes flicking briefly over her with sardonic amusement.

'Tell me, Justin,' he said, in that deep, mellifluous voice. 'Is it customary for members of your company to barge into your office unasked?'

Justin glared, his eyes uncharacteristically angry. 'What are you doing here, Cressida?' he asked briefly.

Cressida, regretting her impetuosity more by the second, turned and spoke directly to Justin, ignoring Stefano completely. 'I'd like to speak to you, please, Justin. Alone,' she added pointedly.

Justin half rose from his seat, his face tight with anger. 'Well, you can't see me. I happen to be in the middle of an important and confidential meeting with Signor di Camilla and I do not appreciate members of the cast bursting in here uninvited with their trifling little complaints—'

'But—'

'It reflects well neither on me, nor on the company. If you want to see me, Cressida, you do it through the proper channels and make an appointment through my secretary. Now would you please excuse us?'

Stefano's eyes glinted, but he said nothing, and Cressida was forced to retreat, feeling thoroughly chastened. But by the time she had returned to her dressing-room, her anger had returned in force, and she sat fuming, the knowledge that she *had* over-stepped the mark by bursting into Justin's office only increasing the rage she felt towards Stefano.

She was biting at the edge of her fingernail, when there was a familiar tap on the door, and she flung it open to find him standing there carelessly, looking as if he hadn't a care in the world, wearing a wonderfully cut suit which had astonishingly escaped being cov-ered in any of the grime from backstage. His sardon-ically handsome face sent her blood-pressure soaring. The insult burst out before she could stop it. 'You bastard!' she hissed.

He stepped back in a gesture of mock alarm, putting one finger over his mouth. 'Ssh,' he murmured. 'Everyone will hear you, and that you don't want, do you? If you're going to insult me, then you had better do it in private.' And he swiftly stepped inside her dressing-room, shut the door, and then leaned against it, surveying her coolly, but with some unholy humour lighting the dark eyes. 'Unless, of course,' he mur-mured, 'you'd prefer to get whatever is obviously bothering you out of your system some other way. You look, *cara*—' he smiled '—as if you would like to do me violence.'

'So I would!' she retorted, and saw the light in his eyes intensify.

'So hurt me,' he challenged, his narrowed eyes on her mouth. 'Do you want to slap my face? Hmm? Would that make you feel better?' His voice lowered to become a deep, velvet caress. 'Or do I know some-thing else that would make you feel better still?'

It was as though he were choreographing her response, she thought desperately as she fought and failed to control her body's reaction to him. She felt the shaming springing into life of her nipples, their peaks growing tauter by the second, pushing insistently against the cotton of the shirt she wore, sending him their message of want just as clearly as if she'd written it down on a piece of paper and handed it to him. Blood flared in her cheeks, and she could feel every pulse-point in her body beating out in insistent demand, the beats growing faster and stronger with every second that passed. How was it possible to hate a man so much, and yet want him with a fervent fire which excluded the rest of the world?

She forced a deep breath into her lungs, knowing that his discerning eyes would have missed nothing, and as she caught a glimpse of herself in the mirror over his shoulder she saw that even her eyes betrayed her, with their huge blackened centres leaving only the thinnest rim of colour showing. 'Why are you doing this? Just tell me why, Stefano—and I'll try to understand!'

Two hands were held in the air in question. 'What?'

'Don't you "what?" me!' she erupted. 'First you barge back into my life and finance the play. That in itself is laughable—you haven't one artistic bone in the whole of your body.'

'No?' he queried, laughing.

She shot him a look of pure venom. 'You hate the theatre.'

'Maybe I've changed?'

'And pigs might fly!' She took another breath. 'If all *that* weren't bad enough, you then take it upon yourself to start abusing your power by making changes which simply won't work!'

'What are you talking about?'

'Oh, don't play the innocent with me, Stefano! I know you, and I know how you like to work. And to satisfy your stupid, chauvinistic power-trip you've just jeopardised the whole play.'

The light had died in the ebony depths, leaving his eyes as expressionless as if they had been forged of some dark, cold metal. 'I think that you'd better explain what exactly it is that you're accusing me of,' he said, in a dangerously quiet voice.

'The play!' she stormed. 'The first act! You've ordered David to rewrite it.'

'I've ordered David to rewrite it,' he repeated slowly.

'You couldn't bear it, could you? You couldn't bear to see me getting my acting together, could you? Just when I'm starting to make something of myself you decide to callously ruin it. This is the first West-End play I've ever been in—do you know what that means to an actress? Do you?' She saw his mouth tighten and an uncharacteristic paleness lighten his smooth olive complexion.

'Tell me more.' His voice was harsh, the accent pronounced.

She gave him a withering look. 'Do you want me to spell out the damage you've probably done? The play was good as it stood. It worked. Audiences like glamorous settings and they like to hear the sound of the sea—it's a device which *works*. And just because you didn't like me showing my figure off in a swimsuit is not a good enough reason to order the scene to be rewritten.'

'What?' His query was an incredulous murmur.

'David may now be yet another of your tame puppets, but I'm not, and I'm telling you to use your influence to change it back to what it was before. Speaking of which, I'd like to know just what you *did* say to David—as he barely spoke to me this morning? And finally—' her voice had died, along with her breath '—I am no longer your possession. There's nothing wrong with my body, and I'm not ashamed of being on stage in a swimsuit—and even if I decided to run on wearing nothing but a fig-leaf it has absolutely *nothing to do with you!*'

'Attempt to do that and you'll never act again,' he told her, with a grim certainty that she didn't doubt for a moment, his eyes fixing her with a baleful stare which sent a shiver down her spine.

She had been goaded into saying things that she didn't mean. She had meant to retaliate, true, but the look of pure fury which distorted his face showed her that she had far exceeded her objective. She opened her mouth to back down a little, when a rat-tat-tat on the door broke into the tension.

'Hi, Cressy!' called David's cheerful voice.

Cressida looked at Stefano before she could stop herself, and then angrily realised that she was looking to him to take the lead. But his next words astonished her.

'Let him in,' he said softly.

'But you're in here,' she reasoned, her independence reasserting itself. 'What if he thinks—?'

'Let him in,' he repeated quietly.

Hating herself as she did so, she obeyed him, finding no comfort from David's wide smile.

He peered into the dressing-room. 'Oh, hello, Stefano,' he said pleasantly, and Cressida could have cheerfully kicked him.

'What can I do for you, David?' she asked him in frozen formal tones.

David seemed totally oblivious to the tension in the small room. 'I just wanted to say that I hoped you liked the changes I made. I meant to let you know about them beforehand, but I was busy writing them, and what with one thing and another…'

Cressida stared at him, and then turned her head so that she could see triumphant black eyes mocking her from the mirror. '*You* decided on the changes?' she asked uncertainly.

David looked slightly bemused. 'Yes, of course I decided on them. Justin thought that the pace of the story could be improved and he ordered them. Why, who on earth else did you think would have anything to do with them?'

Stefano's mocking voice sizzled as he spoke. 'Yes, Cressida,' he echoed. 'Just who?'

She felt an utter fool. 'I wasn't really thinking straight,' she muttered.

'Oh, really? And why was that?' The voice was perfectly controlled, the Italian accent scarcely apparent.

'Would you both please excuse me?' Before I do something stupid like break down and cry.

'Of course,' said David immediately. 'I'll see you later.'

His departure was as unnoticeable as his arrival,

thought Cressida, her head bent, unwilling to face Stefano. But one thing was for sure—she owed him an apology. 'I'm sorry,' she said. 'I shouldn't have lost my temper like that...' But he silenced her with a small sound which almost bordered on gentleness, and which had the most ridiculous effect on her. She felt tears prick at her eyes.

'Shush,' he urged her. 'Look at me.'

She shook her head, the dark red plait swaying either side of the slender neck.

'Cressida?'

She looked up then, her gaze defiant, her over-bright eyes giving her away.

'Tears, Cressida?' he whispered. '*Tears*?'

'I'm under a lot of stress,' she managed, which was true, but not the reason for this over-emotional display. It was him. He was the reason. 'Now would you please go, Stefano? Please?'

His eyes were darkly enigmatic. 'Of course I will go, but only if you promise me that you will stop looking so sad. Why would you not have considered me responsible? It was perfectly natural to do so. But now you know that I am not the—how do you say?—''villain of the piece'', yes?'

'You know it is.' She laughed in spite of herself. It had been another of his traits which she had found so endearing, this helpless Latin approach, fumbling to master a colloquialism when they both knew perfectly well that he spoke English as well as she did.

'Well, then. Now that you know this, is it not easier if we continue as friends, rather than enemies?'

Her mind froze as it locked on that single word. 'Friends?' she repeated.

His smile was sardonic. 'Why not?'

Why not? He really had no idea, she thought sadly. *Friends.* The word mocked her with its curiously impartial ring. For yes, she had hoped once, in her naïveté, that perhaps things could be amicable between them. In those early days of the separation—when she had lain awake at night, telling herself that leaving him had been her only option, like an incantation which if she chanted enough she might some day believe—she had thought that things might one day be 'civilised' between them. But never friends. Instinctively she had recognised then that the neutrality of friendship could never be more than a wild dream—and now she knew it for a fact.

How could she befriend a man who sent her thoughts and her senses into such chaotic confusion? A man who only had to pull her into his arms to make her respond with an overwhelming passion whose source she dared not question too closely.

But Stefano shared none of these weaknesses. He wanted her as a friend, albeit a friend he still desired physically—he had admitted that—but nothing more than that.

''What are you so afraid of?' he asked softly.

Self-respect forced her to adopt a careless smile, for how humiliating if he even began to guess at the turmoil of her emotions where he was concerned, and to turn him down would surely be to give him some hint of that.

For her own sake, and for the sake of the company, she should *try*. After all, the cessation of hostilities just might lessen the tension and the strain between them.

She stared into the dark eyes, narrowed as they studied her.

'So? Are we friends?'

She nodded. 'All right.'

'And are friends allowed to have dinner?'

She shook her head. 'Stefano, no.'

He shrugged. 'But why? What are you afraid of?'

The same question the same answer.

If only you knew. I'm afraid of you, she thought, or, more importantly, me. The way I can't seem to control my feelings when you're around me. She put her fingertips on her mouth as she stared back at him, as though to block any words she was afraid she might speak. Yet wasn't it the adult thing to do—to calmly agree and say 'yes'? And there was curiosity, too. How had he changed? How would it make her feel, to sit opposite him, alone together in a restaurant after all this time?

'So is it "yes"?'

The last of her doubts was silenced by some mischievous demon in her heart. 'OK,' she agreed. 'When?'

He raised his eyebrows a fraction. 'Why, tonight, of course. When else?'

CHAPTER SEVEN

I MUST be *mad*, thought Cressida, as she scrubbed furiously at her hair under the rather inefficient splutter of warm water which came from the ancient shower. She had actually agreed to have supper with Stefano, after agreeing that they should try to be 'friends'. Friends? She squirted some conditioner on to the palm of her hand and rubbed it into her scalp. A friend would never arrogantly presume that she was free to have dinner with him *that night*.

And did she really think that they could really sit companionably like two civilised people in the public arena of a restaurant, when in the past they'd almost come to blows in similar circumstances in the final stages of their ill-fated marriage?

But then some devil within her made her stop and think again, and she found herself remembering her ability to make him laugh—with her impressions of two very famous American film stars. Stefano—serious, powerful Stefano—sitting listening to her, his shoulders shaking in silent laughter.

She stepped out of the shower. Think about the bad times, she urged herself as she pulled on a towelling robe and wrapped her hair up in a turban to dry. But somehow, tonight, those bad memories were stubbornly slow in coming. If she had any sense, she would cancel right now.

Should she attempt to ring him? Tell him she'd changed her mind? She shook her head a little, as if someone else in the room had asked the question. She knew Stefano well enough, and he was not a man to tolerate indecision. A *frisson* of apprehension ran down the length of her shower-dampened spine as she realised the futility of any such insurrection—knowing full well that if she told him she had changed her mind about dinner he simply would not take 'no' for an answer.

Sighing, she pulled open her wardrobe door, comforting herself with the fact that the abandonment of hostilities could only be good for the company at large.

She recognised with a sinking heart that her pulse had accelerated to a dangerously high level. She had never felt this way when David was due to collect her. And why had the choice of which outfit to wear suddenly become of paramount importance? Because it's *him*, you fool, whispered a mocking voice. Him, always him—and you always felt this way about him.

She pulled the tie of her bathrobe tighter around her slender waist, silently remonstrating with herself. You are *not* out to impress him, she thought. He has women galore, and you are no longer one of them. And if she wore anything which even remotely suggested that she had dressed to please him, knowing Stefano as she did, it would be an invitation he would not resist. She closed her eyes as she envisaged him responding to any such invitation.

Stop it, she thought. Just stop it. You're an actress—

and you, of all people, should surely be able to convince Stefano that you are no longer someone whom he can manipulate by the sheer force of his personality and sexuality. Convincing him might be possible, she concluded as she pulled on some silky white panties; convincing herself might pose an altogether different challenge.

In the end she settled for an outfit which she hoped would cover all contingencies—it most definitely did not scream 'come and get me', and yet it was well made enough to be one in the critical eye for Stefano, hopefully convincing him that, although she lived frugally, she certainly didn't dress like a pauper. It was a classically cut and beautifully simple dress in softest jersey. In emerald-green, it accentuated the much darker green of her eyes, its skirt swirling around her narrow hips, the bodice clinging discreetly to the high curve of her breasts. She wore a minimum of make-up—dusting her eyelids with the merest hint of green frosting, a pale sheen of pink outlining the full curve of her mouth. She let the newly washed dark red hair cascade down, and it fell in a gleaming cloud around her shoulders.

Hastily buffing up her black shoes and matching clutch bag, she was ready just in time to hear the doorbell. She had protested that she could get to any restaurant in London under her own steam, but, true to form, she had protested in vain. Stefano had overridden everything, other than his determination that she should travel with him, and in his car.

She pulled the door open, and a curious feeling of shyness suddenly enveloped her. Her heart caught in her mouth as she stared back at him. He looked—he just looked like Stefano, she acknowledged with an almost wistful wryness. In other words—an absolute knock-out.

Was it because he was Italian that he wore clothes with such consummate ease? Or was it just him? The grey suit was fashionably loose, and yet it left none of his very masculine attributes in any doubt. The muscular length of his thigh was instantly discernible, as was the broad chest in the fine shirt, and the taut flatness of his stomach beneath the leather belt he wore.

Her mouth suddenly dry, she croaked out, 'Hello,' from between parched lips, furious with herself for automatically moistening them with her tongue, seeing his eyes darken in amused response.

'Hello to you,' he murmured. 'Ready?'

It was stupid that she should feel disappointed that he hadn't complimented her on her appearance. She made to grab her coat from the hook, but he pre-empted her and an olive-skinned hand moved in the direction of the hook. But he raised dark eyebrows when he saw that it was the duffel coat.

'This?' he asked disbelievingly.

She stuck a mutinous chin in the air. 'There's nothing wrong with it,' she said defiantly. 'I'm very fond of it.'

'You must be,' he said, sarcasm apparent in the deep voice, and then anger. 'Why, Cressida? Why do you wear such garments? I bought you coats, many coats—a million times better than this—and yet you left them behind and instead elect to walk around like a tramp. Why?'

'You bought clothes for your pretty toy,' she retorted. 'Another gift to foist on her, to keep her quiet. Candy for the baby. I preferred to buy my own clothes—they represented an independence I thought I'd lost forever.'

'I see.' His mouth twisted as he surveyed the tattered coat, moving to stare at the wall where a corner of the ugly flocked wallpaper had peeled away from it. 'And was it worth it, this independence? The price wasn't too high?'

'I don't think of things in terms of price,' she replied, knowing that she was evading the question—for how he would laugh if he discovered that acting was, for her, a job she did and enjoyed, but not with the burning passion it was for someone like, say, Jenna— a passion that she'd once convinced herself that she shared.

She stared up at him. 'There's little point in us having dinner if we're going to spend the whole time arguing. Perhaps—'

But he cut across her suggestion by smoothly holding the duffel coat up for her to slip her arms into, his face relaxed, affable and charming. And dangerous as hell, she reminded herself, furiously recognising that he was right and wishing that she *had* a wrap in warm, soft cashmere to throw over her dress, instead of looking like an overgrown student!

With her studiously walking a few steps behind him, they made their way downstairs and outside, to where the luxurious lines of his dark, expensive car looked completely out of place in the fairly ordinary neighbourhood in which she lived.

He insisted on closing her door for her, in the old-fashioned, protective way which had once so charmed her. Her eyes went sightlessly to the window as the engine purred smoothly into power. She was going to get absolutely nowhere if she allowed herself to dwell on the past all evening, on how it had been. This is how it is *now*, she reminded herself. It's over. You were totally unsuited. Stefano wanted a 'yes' woman—someone to moan in his bed, and look beautiful at his dinner table. He was, and is, an out-and-out chauvinist who lured you into marriage making you believe you were going to be equals, and then proceeded to shut you out of his life, leaving you feeling isolated and unloved. Never forget all that.

'So serious,' mused the deep voice. 'What is it that you say—"a penny for them"?'

She stole a glance at the perfect but hard profile. Once her lips would have twitched irresistibly at this. But not now. 'You know perfectly well that it is, but no, I have no intention of telling you what's going on inside my head. You wouldn't be flattered,' she said, as an afterthought.

'I can imagine,' he said coldly.

Cressida's fingers drummed helplessly against the patent leather of her clutch bag as the limousine drew up outside what was obviously the restaurant, although it didn't advertise the fact from the outside. 'Oh, this is hopeless,' she protested. 'Why ever did we imagine that things could be any different? We still fight like cat and dog.'

The dark eyes mocked her. 'Then let's not.'

'Maybe we can't,' she said quietly, her eyes downcast.

'Maybe,' he said softly, and something in the way he spoke made her turn her eyes to meet him, to be dazzled by their steely light. 'But I know one arena where we never fought, don't you, Cressida?'

She knew immediately what he meant. She shook her head desperately, afraid. Terrified that she would sink into his arms, seduced by the rich velvet of his voice, and by her memories of how wonderful that particular arena of which he spoke had been. And hadn't that been a major problem—that bed had been their only arena, that he had carefully excluded her from all the other sides of his life? Her hands were shaking badly, but to her surprise he merely placed one strong, warm hand over both, to cover them. The gesture was brief, but the sensation of the contact was electrifying and she quickly pulled her hands away as though something had stung her, not wanting him to see that she could still behave like some gauche young schoolgirl around him.

She saw his mouth tighten as he ushered her into the restaurant, where the head waiter materialised instantly out of the gloom.

They were seated at the best table. It was a long time since she had been anywhere as lovely as this, and she glanced round the room like someone trying to re-establish a landmark. She recalled Alexia's comment about the women in the restaurant looking as though they'd like to eat Stefano. Well, the women in *this* restaurant obviously had similar appetites, she decided with a stab of something which felt uncomfortably like jealousy. Glittering, beautiful women who were eyeing him with an open greed which made her flesh creep. Stefano, on the other hand, didn't seem to have noticed at all, unconcernedly scanning the leather-bound menu which the waiter had handed to them. But he was aware, of course; Cressida knew that. His mother had pointed out that he had had a devastating effect on members of the opposite sex since before he was out of his teens.

She looked at her own menu, but could make little sense of the words. Doing something as mundane as choosing food seemed almost laughable when she felt so on edge, overpoweringly aware of the man opposite her.

'What would you like to eat?'

She swallowed. 'I don't know if I'm even hungry.'

'You will be when you see the food. Let me order for you.'

It was the kind of arrogant male assumption which she had convinced herself she detested, and David would never have presumed to choose her meal for her, and yet she found herself nodding. 'OK.'

The restaurant was French, and their waiter obviously new and eager, but he was trying much too hard. His enthusiasm for each item on the menu was almost farce-like, and when he shook Cressida's napkin out and a knife fell to the floor he was abject in his apologies to Stefano.

And, unbidden, as the waiter apologetically replaced it, Cressida's gaze met Stefano's and there was a second of shared but amused resignation. Stefano was irritated by the waiter, Cressida knew that, though she doubted that the waiter himself or anyone else in the restaurant also knew it. Because he would be kind to the waiter. Ruthless in business, he was always kind to the 'little people' who worked for him, she had seen it countless times, treating them with a politeness which always produced a fierce loyalty.

The waiter gone, he looked at her, his long fingers closed together as though in prayer, the strong chin resting on them.

'We're not eating Italian, then?' she asked, in some surprise.

He laughed. 'You accuse me of being partisan, is that it, Cressida?'

'I'm surprised that you didn't take me to the Scala,' she challenged.

Dark eyebrows winged arrogantly upwards. 'Oh?'

'Alexia said…' She stopped.

'Yes?' he queried softly. 'What did Alexia say?'

'She said it's the best Italian restaurant in London.'

'Did she?' He looked amused. 'Well, she is wrong. It is good, but not, I would say, the best.'

'Did you sleep with her?' The words were out before she could stop them, and she stared back at him, appalled.

'That's really none of your business,' he said coldly.

Her voice didn't waver one bit. 'No, you're quite right. It isn't.'

The dark eyes had narrowed and were staring at her consideringly. 'As a matter of fact, I didn't. Just because a woman makes herself available doesn't automatically mean that a man has to assuage himself. Does it?' he mocked.

As she, Cressida, had done, that very first night at her flat? And if Stefano had not stopped, she would have let him take her, virgin or not, right then and there, standing up, with her back pressed against the wall.

Dull, shameful colour rushed into her cheeks, but just then the waiter arrived with their first course. It was artichoke—messy but delicious—and she was glad that eating it required all her attention.

Stefano immersed one of the leaves into the melted butter, gently tearing at the flesh with his teeth, and she did the same.

'So, Cressida—how are your family? Your parents are still the hippies? Dropping out, mmm?'

She nodded. 'Afraid so. I went to see them last summer.'

'And how was it?'

'Odd.'

'Why "odd"?'

She shrugged. 'I felt like the parent, and they the children.' She remembered how ridiculous they had both looked, with their long greying hair, the faded clothes and the beads. And yet the love she felt for them had not been diminished by their eccentricities. She remembered telling them about her failed marriage, that it was over, and that she no longer loved Stefano. 'I don't believe you,' her mother had said flatly. 'Your eyes come alive when you speak of him.'

Cressida shook her head, coming back to the present, realising that all avenues of thought seemed to lead to this man.

She searched around for a neutral topic. 'And your own family?' she asked politely.

He dipped long brown fingers into the finger-bowl at his side and dried them on his napkin. 'They are well. My mother, naturally enough, is anxious for me to produce an heir. But in order to do that, I must first settle down.'

Cressida bent her head over the finger-bowl, concentrating fiercely on the piece of lemon which floated there, totally unprepared for the sick feeling of jealousy which flooded through her, but determined that he should not witness it. It was several moments before she felt sufficiently composed to meet his eyes. 'Oh, really?' she enquired, somehow managing to keep her voice neutral. 'Has she—anyone in mind?'

He shrugged. 'But naturally. It is one of the disadvantages of being a soon-to-be single—' he hesitated on the word '—man, that mothers and sisters constantly parade what they consider to be ''suitable'' would-be partners.'

And *that* was why he was reluctant to divorce her— he had admitted it. Because their 'marriage' protected him from such women. She looked down at the heavy silver fork, wondering what would happen if she smashed it down on her side-plate, to shatter it into a thousand pieces. 'Some disadvantage,' she said coldly. 'That sounds like the kind of disadvantage that most men would give their eye-teeth for.'

'Most men, yes.' He paused deliberately. 'I prefer to do my own hunting.'

She wondered just what prompted the self-destructing urge which forced her next question. 'And do you have anyone in mind?' she asked casually. 'For the honour of bearing your child?' But this time when she met his gaze she was startled by the look of naked rage which fleetingly burned on the handsome features.

'Would you care so little?' he bit out. 'Are you really such a cold-hearted, unfeeling little—?'

'Seems I've picked a good moment,' came a smoky American voice. 'Is this a private fight, or can anyone join in?'

Cressida was stunned into silence, but Stefano was instantly on his feet, his arms on the woman's bare forearms, his dark head bending forward to kiss each cheek in the Continental fashion.

'Ebony!' he said warmly.

Ebony! thought Cressida maliciously. What a preposterous name! Even if it did suit her.

At only a few inches below Stefano in height, the woman must have been nearly six feet tall, with the tanned, silky skin and the proud physique of an Amazon. Her eyes were the colour of dark chocolate, but it was her hair which was her most amazing feature—stark jet in colour, it rippled to her waist in a stunning waterfall of black silk. She had her red-fingernailed hand resting lightly on Stefano's arm, a Stefano who normally disliked casual contact, yet did not seem to mind this in the least.

After a few lines of laughing conversation which thoroughly excluded her, Stefano suddenly seemed to remember she was there.

'Ebony,' he said. 'Meet Cressida. Cressida, this is Ebony—you may have seen her on this month's cover of *Vogue*.'

The chocolate eyes had narrowed. 'Cressida?' she said questioningly, and then a cold, hard look came into her eyes.

'Cressida's an actress,' explained Stefano, and Cressida put her hands underneath the table so that they wouldn't see them shaking. An actress, he had said, not his wife. An actress. Perhaps he was in love with the striking model? Perhaps the protection of his marital status held no lure where she was concerned.

'Oh?' drawled Ebony. 'An actress? Have I seen you in anything?'

'I'm about to open in *All or Nothing* at the Carlisle, and I did a couple of commercials on television last year,' said Cressida quietly, and without emotion.

There was a short silence, broken by Ebony.

'Well,' she smiled, and there was a question in her eyes as she looked directly at Stefano. 'Seems like I'm *de trop* here. I'll see you tomorrow, Stefano, huh?' And with two more small kisses, she was gone, undulating like some magnificently exotic snake, the eyes of every man in the restaurant upon her.

Stefano resumed his seat and regarded her carefully. 'And do you want to ask me any questions?' he mocked.

Sadness fought with jealousy. Don't let him *see* that you care, urged an inner voice. 'Why should I?' she said calmly. 'You seem to know each other very well.'

He leaned back in his chair. 'Yes,' he agreed. 'Perhaps even better than you seem to know David, Cressida.'

The implication of this statement filled her with a cold, sick feeling, and Cressida suddenly knew that she could not endure one second more of this torture— for torture it was.

She *had* been mad to come tonight, an innocent, self-deluding fool. She pushed her chair back. 'I'm sorry, Stefano, but I don't think that this was such a good idea. This meal was a mistake, and I can't sit here and work my way through another two courses. I'm sorry. I want to go home.'

To her surprise, he made no demur, calmly asking for the bill and insisting on paying for the uneaten meal. Cressida saw the look of surprise on the faces of the other diners, but Stefano calmly guided her towards the door as if he couldn't care less. She realised that a lot of men—David, for instance—would have found it embarrassing to curtail a meal like this. But Stefano, she thought wryly, was not, as he had pointed out to her himself, most men.

The journey home was silent and seemed to Cressida to take forever. The tension in the large car was almost palpable, and she was ridiculously over-aware of his presence beside her. They used to ride home from the theatre like this, she thought, discussing what they'd just seen—and, finding the servants gone home for the night, they would make love and then Stefano would prepare a midnight feast for them both, bringing crusty bread and omelette and wine into their bed, and they would giggle like naughty school-children as the crumbs fell on to the linen sheets.

But why remember that tonight? Especially tonight, when she had been confronted with the evidence of the woman in his life. Could Judy be right—could she still be in love with the man?

Misery swamped over her as the powerful car slid to a halt outside her flat.

'Shall I see you inside?' It was a curt, cold question.

'No, thank you,' she said formally, marvelling that the small, frozen voice was really hers.

She dragged open the car door and ran to the front door of her flat, praying that he wouldn't see the tears which were starting to spill from her eyes, aware that the long, sleek car remained there, unmoving, before she slammed the door shut behind her.

She made it to the sofa like a wounded animal,

whimpering little sobs tearing at her throat as she realised how naïve her question had been. Because tonight
she had realised that her mother had been right: she
had not been living since she had left Stefano—not
living at all, but existing, a safe, but dead little existence.

He had breathed fire and life into her again; she was
nothing but an empty shell without him.

And only a self-deluding fool would deny what she
now knew to be the truth. That she loved Stefano. Of
course she did. She had never really stopped.

And her eyelids fluttered to spread tears all over her
cheeks, as the memory of words he had spoken to her
so long ago began to overwhelm her...

CHAPTER EIGHT

'I LOVE you.'

Cressida stared at the darkly handsome man who stood before her, disbelief clouding her eyes. 'What?'

He smiled. 'I love you.'

She gave a small sound of delight, before hurling herself into his arms, holding her fingers up to his mouth to be kissed. And as she gazed up into the flinty eyes, she recognised with a maturity far beyond her nineteen years that it was the first time he had ever spoken those words. 'Oh, Stefano—I love you, too— so much. I can't believe that you feel the same way— it's like a fairy story.'

'I somehow find it hard to believe myself.' He laughed wryly. 'The thunderbolt has hit me. Temptress,' he whispered, and kissed her, his hand moving to cup the swelling breasts, his other hand clasped in the richness of her hair. She gave a small moan as the familiar warmth began to build inside her, her small hands running down the muscular wall of his chest, but he, as he had done on every other occasion, removed her hand, put it back to his lips, and kissed it again.

'Oh,' she protested. 'No.' He was always in control, and sometimes she resented it. However wonderful their lovemaking, he always possessed the will-power to draw back, almost as though he was slightly detached from the passion which threatened to engulf her.

'Oh,' he mimicked. 'Yes.' And then suddenly his eyes became soft, as did his voice. 'We must be married, *cara*. And soon. For I cannot wait much longer.'

They had known each other less than three months and she couldn't believe what she'd heard. 'Married?' she echoed.

'But of course. To feel like this is too rare to squander. I had—' he spoke quietly, as if to himself '—doubted the existence of such feelings.' He turned her hand over to move his mouth sensually over the palm, to trace tiny erotic paths with the tip of his tongue, sending shivers down to every nerve-ending. 'I do not want an affair with you, Cressida—I want you to be my wife.'

She was nineteen and, with all the brash confidence of youth, said the first thing that came into her head. 'But what about my career?'

The dark eyes glinted as he bent his head to place his lips at the soft hollow of her neck. 'Your career?' he whispered. 'Careers are the last thing on my mind at this moment, *cara*.'

'No, I'm serious!' She laughed.

'And so am I. You have almost finished your course. You can work as much or as little as you like. We'll live in London during the week, and in Italy from Friday through to Sunday. You can fit your work around that. Now, does that make you happier?'

'Quite happy,' she said breathlessly.

'And what would make you even happier?' he mused. 'This?' And his mouth found her neck again.

He pushed the curtain of hair aside and kissed the line of her jaw, moving so carelessly towards her mouth that she moved restlessly in his arms. His face hovered over hers for a second, the dark eyes hooded, the lips enticing, humour lifting the corners as he registered the longing in her half-parted lips. Just millimetres away, he stayed there, so that anticipation grew like a wind-fanned flame, and at the same time his hand moved lightly down her spine, and further, to cup her buttocks, pulling her against him so that she could feel the throbbing hardness of his arousal, and her pupils darkened as she gazed back at him, dizzy with love and longing.

'I want you to be my wife,' he repeated huskily.

'Oh, darling, yes. I love you, I love you. Please— oh, Stefano, *oh*,' she gasped as he began to kiss her with relentless intent.

But he had not made love to her until their wedding night, and the weeks before had been an agony. Cressida had found herself veering between admiration and resentment at his iron-hard control—the way in which he could bring himself back from the edge of the abyss to douse the fires of their passion.

Taking her aunt with them—her parents would join them directly from Ibiza—they flew out to be married in Italy on her twentieth birthday in a dark, splendid church surrounded by what seemed like hundreds of his relatives, who eyed Cressida as though she were some alien from another planet. The rain had been torrential, with the sound of thunder and lightning drowning the incantations of the priest. Even covered by an umbrella, Cressida had been soaked running to the car, the silk of her gown clinging to her body like wet tissue-paper, the tulle of her veil transformed from a billowing cloud to a limp, sodden rag.

But after the reception he had driven her through the tortuously twisting mountain roads to a tiny remote cabin, and once inside he had just stood for a moment, staring at her, a strange light in his eyes, before holding his arms wide open with the simple command, 'Come,' and she had run to him, breathless with anticipation, and longing, and love.

She had thought that after the long wait it would all happen very quickly, but she was wrong. He kissed her and told her how much he loved her and settled her with a glass of wine while he built an enormous fire which filled the cabin with its warmth and sent orange and black shadows licking at the walls.

And finally he came to her again, holding her tightly in his arms before slowly removing all her clothes— her smart honeymoon suit, the silk stockings and the wispy underwear bought specially for him—with such an expression of ardour on his face that she felt as though she would die of love for him.

He took so long to prepare her, pleasuring her with his hands and mouth, that the pain was far more fleeting than she had been given to believe, and as he felt her tense with it she stared directly into his eyes, seeing fierce pride burning there, and then he began to move inside her, bringing her at last to a heart-stopping crescendo as she fell over the edge to fulfilment.

And they had spent three weeks in that cabin—the most wonderful three weeks of her life. Discovering each other. Long walks, and scratch meals and log fires. And love. Especially love.

* * *

Cressida rubbed her temples as she awoke from yet another troubled sleep, trying to dispel the dull ache in her head. A tension headache, they called it. And yet she had not seen Stefano. Not since the night when they'd had dinner. When...She bit her lip. When she had, during some crazed brainstorm, decided that she was still in love with him. Had he deliberately been staying away from the theatre since that night?

Perhaps he, too, had recognised the futility of their meeting in an attempt to be 'friends'. But she doubted whether he, like her, had spent the past few nights haunted by images of the past, which filled her with an aching longing.

But it was time to snap out of it. Pointless to re-member the past. The past was a lifetime ago, and so much had happened since then. And to remember love was nothing but a brutal exercise, since she could never even be sure whether Stefano had *really* loved her—for if he had then why had he gradually dis-tanced himself from her, so that eventually she had come to believe that the caring, sharing man of those early days had never really existed?

She let herself out of the flat. She had agreed to meet David for a coffee before rehearsal, and she made her way to the croissant shop near the theatre, so lost in her own thoughts that she barely took in the beauty of the perfect May morning.

David was sitting at a table, an empty coffee-cup in front of him. He stood up as she arrived.

'Cressida!' He leaned forward and kissed her on the cheek. 'What can I get you? Some croissants? Bread?'

She shook her head. 'Just coffee, please, David.'

He frowned. 'You're very thin. Are you eating properly?'

No, I'm not, she thought, as she watched him buy two cups of coffee. I'm not functioning normally at all, and I have Stefano to thank for that. 'Thanks.' She smiled as he placed the coffee before her. 'What did you want to talk to me about?'

He sat opposite her, a slightly sheepish look on his gentle face. 'I don't quite know how to put this,' he said, and Cressida's heart sank for she had a feeling she knew what was coming.

'I know that we haven't been seeing as much of each other as before—'

'That's because—'

'No, please, Cressida—let me finish.' He put his hands, palm down, on the table. 'I don't want to pry into your past—not if you don't want me to. But what I do want, Cressida, is to have a relationship with you. A *real* relationship this time.'

'David, please—'

'Listen to me,' he said. 'I know you're a traditional girl at heart, so if it's marriage you want...?'

He looked at her questioningly, a wistful smile on his lovely, open face, and Cressida felt sick with shame. What would he say if he knew how she'd been behaving with Stefano? She stared back at him in dismay, realising that she would never be able to love another man the way she loved Stefano. And an image of a bleak, solitary future stretched out before her, frightening her with its loneliness.

She put her hand over one of David's, shaking her head gently as she met his eyes. 'You flatter me more than I deserve, David,' she said softly. 'And I'm hon-

oured by what you say—but—I'm so sorry. I can't
marry you, or have a relationship with you, because I
don't feel the same way about you. I think you're a
wonderful man—'

'There's someone else, isn't there?' he asked suddenly.

There was silence for a moment. 'In a way,' she
said at last. 'Please don't ask.'

'I won't. I've got a good idea who it is, but I'll say
nothing. But let me ask you this, Cressida—why be
with a man who makes you look so utterly miserable?'

Because I'm not *with* him, she thought in desperation, as they stood up to leave. That role is filled perfectly by Ebony.

The week before opening dragged on, with still no
sign of Stefano, but by the time the first night arrived
Cressida found herself filled with some of the heady
optimism of the rest of the cast.

'We *can't* fail, lovie. We're going to be brilliant!'
Adrian had laughed as he swung Cressida up in the
air on stage, an hour before the curtain went up. 'Say
after me—''we're the greatest thing since sliced
bread''!'

'We're the greatest thing since sliced bread,' giggled Cressida obediently, her hands on his shoulders,
her head flung back with the silky hair like a flying
red banner. His mood was infectious, and as he lowered her to the floor she saw Stefano over his shoulder,
just standing watching her, the dark, hard face betraying not a flicker of emotion, and her heart turned over
as she acknowledged the impassivity of those regular
features, recognising his indifference towards her.
When they had been married he had been unbelievably

jealous of any man who even looked at her. Observing his coolly neutral demeanour, the lack of anger in his eyes told her more clearly than anything to date so far how little she now meant to him. She swallowed. 'Will you be in the audience tonight?'

'Why?' The voice mocked her. 'Would you care?'

She turned her back to him, afraid that he would read the lie in her eyes. 'Not particularly.' She made as if to move away, but his voice stopped her.

'Cressida…'

She turned round as surely as if he'd spun her by an invisible rope. 'What?'

The dark eyes burned some unfathomable message. 'I'll be there. Watching you.'

And perversely it pleased her to think that he would be there. Perverse because as the atmosphere in the theatre grew, and the tension built up, her thoughts were all for Stefano.

She gave the performance of her life. For him. She wanted to show him what she was capable of.

Her speech at the end of the second act was enthusiastically applauded, and she felt a heady rush of pride. It was a difficult speech at the best of times—with the woman agonising over whether she had driven her husband into the arms of her best friend. Painfully honest—it needed every ounce of emotion to be wrung from it to prevent it from sounding trite. Whenever she spoke it, Cressida felt as though her soul had been stripped bare for all to see, but tonight, knowing that *he* was in the audience, she felt totally drained afterwards.

As she took her bow at the end, she willed herself not to be mesmerised by him, but it was useless; she found her eyes drawn to where he sat beside Justin, colour staining her cheeks as she saw his smile of satisfaction, saw the strong olive-skinned hands applauding.

Still powered by the strong rush of adrenalin, she came backstage for the celebration. Champagne was poured and drunk by most with an almost fervent desperation. Some of the cast would stay until the first editions were off the press, as they waited to hear what the critics would make of the play, but Cressida had already decided that she would go home after a cursory appearance. For once, she felt as though she would be able to sleep.

She stood, drinking mineral water, not in the mood for champagne, when Stefano appeared by her elbow. And he was alone, she noted. No sign of his stunning mistress. He stood looking down at her for a moment, a dark brow lifting in query as he surveyed the contents of her glass.

'You're not drinking?' he observed.

The sight of him in his black dinner-jacket was doing dangerous things to her heart-rate. 'I don't know whether I've got anything to celebrate yet,' she croaked, through lips which were suddenly dry.

'You have,' he said with an air of quiet finality, and she stared into his eyes.

Oh, no, I haven't, she thought silently, the truth as blinding as a neon light. Because none of it was worth it, none of it. She could have been the world's biggest box-office hit, or the toast of Hollywood—but none of it would matter, because she didn't have the only thing which made her life worth living. She didn't have Stefano.

CHAPTER NINE

CRESSIDA stared at her diary. Two more weeks of the play left, that was all. An eight-week run, and she'd completed six of them, which left only two.

Two more weeks and Stefano would be out of her life for good, and before he left perhaps he might agree to the divorce. If only she could feel more enthusiastic about that possibility...

She hadn't seen him at all. He had stayed away from the theatre and she knew that she should be grateful for that, and yet, somehow, not seeing him when she knew he was around was the worst thing of all.

Before she knew it, it was the last week, the last matinée.

'Sad?' asked Adrian, as they waited to go on stage before the very last performance.

'A bit,' she admitted. More than a bit, though the reason was laughable.

'You're coming to the last-night party, of course?'

'Of course,' she echoed. 'It's mandatory for the leading lady to attend, isn't it?'

Adrian's eyebrows were raised. 'You might sound a bit more enthusiastic,' he chided.

'I know. Sorry.' But how could she possibly be enthusiastic when Stefano would probably turn up with Ebony in tow?

Adrian grinned. 'So who's the lucky man?'

She looked at him quickly. 'What do you mean?'

'Who's your partner for the party tonight? David?'

She shook her head. 'No, not David,' she answered quietly. 'I'm coming on my own.'

She came off-stage to the sound of applause ringing in her ears, going directly to her dressing-room to change for the party. Defiantly, she had bought a new dress. Tonight she was going to pull out all the stops. She was going to look her very best. Stefano might be there with his mistress, but tonight let him gaze at his wife, and perhaps feel a momentary regret.

She cleansed her face of the heavy-duty stage make-up and replaced it with her own, smudging silvery frost over the heavy lids of her eyes, her paleness relieved by a dusting of blusher over the high cheek-bones. A sheen of dark red lipstick completed the look, and it added a touch of vulnerability to the full lips.

Her dress was black and sequin-covered, gleaming like a mermaid's tail. It had cost a fortune, the kind of dress which had filled her wardrobe when she'd lived with Stefano. The kind of dress she should never have bought.

But why not? she thought recklessly, her heart beating fast. She hadn't felt this crazy in a long time, and the craziness seemed somehow to help alleviate the dull, persistent ache in her heart whenever she thought of Stefano and the beautiful woman who now shared his life.

The taxi dropped her off at the restaurant and there was a pin-drop silence as she walked in.

'Hey, Cressida! Over here!'

Adrian and Justin leapt to their feet from the far end

and as she walked towards the large table the whole company began clapping and cheering, but Cressida's heart plummeted in disappointment *because Stefano wasn't there*.

What she had intended as a defiant and glittering farewell to him had collapsed like a deflated balloon. She sat down and disconsolately drank half a glass of champagne, when she became aware of someone watching her.

Slowly she raised her head and looked across the crowded room to see Stefano standing at the doorway. In his dinner-jacket he looked darkly powerful, and, before she could stop herself, she scanned the area behind him, looking for signs of Ebony, but there was none.

The noise of the diners retreated, and the only sound became the thunder of blood in her ears. Her heart leapt with crazy excitement as she saw the way in which his burning gaze seared into her. She found herself unable to tear her eyes away, drinking in the sheer magnetism of the man, her mouth suddenly dry, and with her tongue she moistened her bottom lip.

It was an action which seemed to stir him into life, and he began to walk towards their table.

And just as the restaurant had stilled momentarily for Cressida's entrance, so it did now for Stefano's. Except that hers had been contrived, and his was not. It was totally unconscious—that almost animal-like grace of his. Out of the corner of her eye, Cressida could see Alexia tugging at the waist of her dress, in order to expose more cleavage.

Deliberately, she thought, he sat at the furthest place away from her, and ordered Krug all round. But he continued to watch her—a steady observation from beneath the dark, thickly lashed eyes—and, if she had felt on edge before, now it needed every bit of concentration she had just to stop her hands from shaking.

She took a mouthful of the Krug. I love him, she thought with bitter sadness. And I've lost him, she added, recognising that she had simply fled their marriage—running away from the problems instead of facing them together with him. But then, she reminded herself, Stefano had never been a man to discuss problems—even to acknowledge them...

And after tonight she would never see him again.

'Good evening, Cressida.'

Lost in her reverie, she hadn't noticed that he had swapped seats, and was now sitting opposite her, mocking her sentimental thoughts with his formal greeting.

'Hello,' she said lightly.

'Enjoying yourself?'

'Yes—no—I...' Oh, God—now she sounded brain-dead.

'It is always sad when a production comes to an end?' he suggested.

'Yes.' Especially this one.

The dark eyes swept round the table, where the scene had degenerated somewhat. Alexia was perched on Adrian's lap, where they were exchanging giggled whispers.

Stefano's eyes met hers, a gleam lighting their darkness. 'Come on, I'll take you home.'

Green eyes clashed with glittering jet as he voiced what she had longed for, yet dreaded. Common sense demanded that she deny him this. She shook her head. 'I'll get a taxi.'

'Where's your coat?' he enquired, as if she hadn't spoken. She was lost; she was drowning in the intensity of that bright, hard stare. 'I've got a ticket,' she stumbled, handing him the cloakroom stub.

He reappeared minutes later with the cashmere wrap she had borrowed from Judy. 'I see you're not wearing my favourite coat this evening.' His voice mocked her as he reached out a hand to scoop the soft fabric over her shoulders.

'I can manage.' She tried to shrug him off, but he ignored her.

'Relax,' he commanded softly as his hands wrapped the garment around her.

Relax? With his hands brushing against the thin material of her dress, so that her crazed brain started imagining the firm caress unrestricted by fabric, wanting to feel him touching the bare, soft flesh there? A man walking to his execution would feel more relaxed than she did at that precise moment.

He said goodbye and she saw the raised eyebrows of Alexia and Adrian. God only knew what they must think.

As they stepped outside the restaurant with the lamps surrounded by dazzling haloes of light which pierced the black of the night, a few drops of rain began to fall.

'The car is here,' he stated, and she found herself buckled into the front seat before she realised it. She felt as though she were in a state of shock, in a trance—not herself at all. The only thoughts which echoed round and round her head were the knowledge of how much she was going to miss him, of how good it felt to have him next to her again, even though the sheer force of his personality always made her feel almost weak. But oh, how good it felt to be weak again, to let him chivvy her into the car, to close her eyes as she leaned back, the sound of the rain growing in intensity so that it drummed relentlessly on the roof-top.

It was hard to know where reality ended and fantasy began by the time they reached the door of her apartment, and her hands were trembling so much that she fumbled around the keyhole, so that in the end he had to coolly extract the keys from her grasp and smoothly unlock the door.

Once inside, neither made a move to turn the light on. The door of the sitting-room was open and through the uncurtained windows the sky was lit up by the full fury of the storm. This was *déjà vu* with a difference, she thought desperately, as she stared at him with huge eyes, remembering their wedding night when, too, the storm had raged outside. And after tonight, she would never see him again.

She became imbued with the naïveté which had been her hallmark all those years ago. 'Would you—like some coffee?'

He laughed softly. 'Coffee? Oh, *cara*—I think not.' His voice assumed a low, seductive resonance. 'You know what it is that I want, Cressida. What we both want.'

She shook her head. God, give me the strength to resist him, went her silent plea, but strength seemed to be in short supply tonight. 'No. I don't.' She felt frozen by a mixture of fear and excitement as she stared back at him. There was nothing of the 'friend' in him tonight, she realised. She could feel the waves of his desire emanating towards her in the semi-gloom. She could see his eyes glittering like diamonds, their attention caught by the frantic movement of her pulse.

'You don't? Then perhaps I shall have to tell you, my beauty,' he murmured.

Every ounce of assertion had flown, but enough rationality remained for her to know that if she allowed him to do what he suggested then she might as well have signed her own death warrant. 'No,' she said with a last vestige of vehemence. 'No.' And she walked away from him into the sitting-room.

But he followed her until there was nowhere left for her to go. She was cornered, trapped by her own desire, staring up into his shadowed face with a hunger which sickened and dismayed her.

'Oh, yes,' he said quietly, and shrugged his jacket off, hanging it carelessly over the back of the chair. He loosened his silken tie with a practised hand and undid the top button of his shirt.

The tiny triangle of flesh he had exposed sent a renewed wave of longing washing through her, and she was afraid to move for fear that it would demonstrate the melting in her loins which was fast becoming an unbearable ache.

His eyes held her, dark and invading—belying the almost casual tone of his question. 'What do you think I want, Cressida, mmm? Tell me, *cara*.'

'I don't know.'

Her breathy reply caused a tightening of the firm line of his mouth, suddenly highlighted by a bolt of lightning illuminating the room for an instant like the flash of a camera, producing a tableau far more dramatic than anything she had played on stage that night.

'Oh, I think you do,' he murmured. 'I think you know very well. Don't be afraid. Tell me. Tell me what you want. Or do you want me to do it for you?'

She closed her eyes. 'No.'

'Oh, yes. I think so. Because I know only too well, Cressida, that what you want more than anything else in the world right now is for me to kiss you, yes?'

'I...' Her mouth opened, but no words came. His power, his imposing presence, had sucked away any words of resistance. And besides, he spoke nothing more than the truth.

He smiled. 'And as I begin to kiss you, you would like me to take you in my arms, to run my hands down the length of your spine. But not for more than a second. Because just that is driving you crazy, and you want me to move them round, in order that I can touch your breasts, don't you? Touch them and stroke them until I can feel them swell beneath my fingers, mmm? So that their tips grow so hard that you don't know if it's pain or pleasure.'

The image that he was creating with the velvety tones was one of unbearable eroticism, and even as he spoke her body began to respond as though he were actually touching her. She gripped the edge of the table-top to stop herself from swaying, feeling the warmth spreading from her thighs, lancing through every pore like a hot laser beam.

'But soon,' he continued relentlessly, 'you would like me to slip the dress from your shoulders, wouldn't you? So that I would no longer have to caress you through your dress, but could touch your bare flesh. You would like that,' he repeated. 'Wouldn't you?'

Her head tipped forward, like a top-heavy bloom on a stem. She fought to contradict him, to send him away from her, but her body had been denied this for too long—her poor, love-starved body and a heart which cried out for him. For as she looked up and stared into that breathtakingly handsome face she knew that she had never really stopped loving him, or wanting him.

A crash of thunder deafened her and past fused with present as they stared at one another for an eternity.

'Wouldn't you?' he whispered.

And the word came out in spite of all her misgivings. Reluctantly, but as clear as a bell, her acquiescence echoed around the room. 'Yes.'

He gave a long sigh, a lifting of the corner of the beautiful mouth an illustration of his triumph. 'But I'm not going to do that. Because I want you to show me. Show me how much you want me. Play the siren for me, Cressida,' he whispered.

In the throes of his erotic spell she found herself totally lost, drowning in the seductive bidding of the velvet voice, wanting—yes, actually *wanting*—to obey him, to rid herself of these garments which were now just an intrusive barrier to their mutual pleasure. Very slowly, she slid down the zip and let the dress slide to her ankles until she stood before him clad only in the silky teddy which skimmed the milky pale skin of her thighs. She heard him suck in a ragged breath and she knew a moment of real power as she met his eyes. She could see their opaque appraisal of her partially clothed body, mesmerised by the twin thrusting peaks of her breasts swelling against the oyster silk which confined them.

'*Dio*!' his voice swore on a shudder and he closed his eyes briefly. 'Now take the teddy off,' he said, but his voice was unsteady, and that very unsteadiness gave her another heady rush of power.

She lounged back against the wall, her thighs parting very slightly, but she heard his inrush of breath at the movement. 'No,' she said quietly. 'I won't.'

'Take the rest off!' His voice was very soft, but there was a mad, glittering fever burning in his eyes.

She had never seen him so out of control before and exhilaration combined with desire to flood her veins with a sweet sensation. There was to be no going back now, for she wanted Stefano just as much as he wanted her. And, on this mad, stormy night, she would be his once more.

But tonight she would come to him as an equal. She had always revelled in his mastery, but tonight she would demonstrate hers. She had shown him that she could be weak; now let *him* be weak. Let him, too, for this one night, lose every vestige of pride he had.

She adopted a pose of pure provocation, her arms behind her head, pillowing the thick hair and causing her breasts to jut out even further, the thighs parted a fraction more, a half-smile of invitation gleaming from between her slitted eyes.

'You do it,' she said drowsily, in a voice which sounded heavy and slurred. 'You want it off? You take it off.'

He advanced towards her, making a low moaning noise at the back of his throat, almost as though he were some predator moving in for the kill. He stood

towering over her for an instant and she could see the
anger sparking fire in his eyes as he recognised that
she understood how overpowering his desire for her
was. He, who hated to be vulnerable, was as vulnerable now as she'd ever seen him.

But not for long. With one deliberate and sure
movement, he hooked his hand into the lacy top of
the teddy and ripped it in two with a single movement
before roughly removing the tattered fragments and
tossing them aside. There was a moment of stunned
silence as she stood before him totally naked. And
then she heard him swear beneath his breath as he
caught her into his arms and kissed her with a fierce
hunger which ignited the fire of her desire and she
kissed him back with a yearning desperation, her
hands gripping on to his shoulders, afraid that she
might faint with the sheer pleasure of it if she didn't,
the need for his possession building up with insistent
heat, until she felt she might explode with wanting.

Her fumbling fingers found the belt of his trousers
and she undid it with indecent haste, but when she
struggled with the zip which strained over his hardness
he stopped kissing her.

'*Cristo!*' he swore. 'Cressida—no! Stop that right
now, before I—'

She ignored him, her need as overpowering as his,
some primeval urge to be possessed driving her on.
The zip rasped down with difficulty and she freed him,
unwittingly murmuring her shocked appraisal of how
aroused he was. His arm round her waist, his mouth
biting sweetly at one swollen nipple, he pushed her
back until her bare buttocks were sitting on the edge
of the table.

His hand moved her thighs apart, his fingers finding a velvety moistness which caused the briefest of smiles to play on his mouth before he pushed her back on to the table. She knew the briefest moment of heady anticipation as she felt his hardness moving next to her, and then, with one fierce movement, he pushed into her, and she gasped as fleeting pain soared into breathtaking pleasure as she was filled by him.

He must have felt her tense, for, his hands still straddling her hips, he lifted his head from her breast to stare down at her, his eyes glittering with pleasure.

'So,' he breathed triumphantly. 'No one else. There has been no one else, has there, Cressida?

She gave a small sound of protest. God, that hateful self-control of his—how did he have the steely will to interrogate her at a time like this? 'Don't stop,' she whispered.

'Has there?' he breathed against her mouth.

'No.' And then she sobbed as he moved hard inside her with harsh, unremitting power—driving her on and on until, so unbelievably quickly, far too quickly, she felt the exquisite waves of release wrenching at her womb and her head fell back as she cried out his name, and she felt one last, all-encompassing thrust as he groaned his own fulfilment into the dampness of her neck and her arms tightened around him.

He said nothing for several minutes, and neither did she. He was having difficulty controlling his breath, and she was too busy clinging on to him, not wanting him to withdraw and distance himself from her as he'd done so often in the past. An earthy sensation of terrifying strength filled her with a primitive kind of joy, as she felt the dying spasms as the last of his seed pumped into her.

He raised his head at last and stared down at her, and she saw a wry smile twist at his mouth. 'So,' he said at last, 'does it please you to see me lose all control? To take you with all the haste of a young boy, with my clothes still around my ankles?'

She closed her eyes. Analysis was the last thing she wanted. She wanted to recapture that exquisite pleasure once more. She wanted him to make love to her, over and over again. She had this one night with him, and she wanted nothing to mar it. She opened her eyes to gaze at him solemnly and she couldn't stop herself from lifting up one slender finger to trace the fullness of his bottom lip. He caught the finger between strong white teeth and licked it in the most erotic way possible. 'I...I...' Her voice tailed off, embarrassed.

He laughed softly. 'What is it, *cara mia*?' he prompted, his eyes gleaming.

Tonight she was his equal, and to declare her love for him would be to topple that delicate balance of equality. But with her body she could love him. 'I want you,' she murmured, and she felt him stir inside her.

He carried her like that to the bedroom, with them still locked intimately, but he eased himself out of her as he laid her down on the bed.

'Oh,' she said disappointedly.

He laughed, white teeth gleaming in the dusky light of the room. 'This time, I'm undressing. Be patient, beauty. The wait will be reward enough. But the time I've removed the last of my clothes you will see just how much...'

She let her eyes trail to the dark line of hair which ran down the flat belly, drinking in the sheer beauty of his nakedness. It had been so long since she had seen the magnificent lines of the sleek and powerful limbs, the long legs and rock-hard thighs which seemed to go on forever, the broad chest which tapered down to narrow hips and firm, strong buttocks. I love you, she thought, as he pulled off his wristwatch to put it on the small locker beside the bed, but then she caught the familiar hooded expression, the lids half concealing the dark eyes, the twist of his mouth telling her nothing other than that he wanted to possess her physically again, and soon.

She felt the bed dip as he moved over her, his legs straddling her, and she couldn't stop herself from reaching out to touch him intimately, but she saw him start a little. Probably with astonishment. She had never dared to take the lead in the past; she had been too inhibited by his obvious experience. He took her hand away and held it against his chest very tightly.

'Don't you like it?' she whispered.

His expression became rueful and he raised her hand from his chest to the warm softness of his mouth. 'Not like it?' He shook his head. '*Cara*, I love it, but this time it's going to last all night—and if you start doing that I may not be able to keep my head. Mmm?'

She closed her eyes as he lowered his mouth to hers. If she tried very hard, she could imagine that the desire which softened his voice could almost have masqueraded as tenderness. And as she gave herself up to his kiss, she discovered that it was actually very easy—to imagine that all the quarrels and the bitterness had never taken place, and that this wasn't now, it was then—when Stefano loved her, too.

Dawn filtered in greyly through the windows, through eyelids which were so sleepy that they felt as though they'd been glued together. Cressida struggled to open her eyes, a smile of blissful fulfilment on her mouth as memory seeped back. When Stefano had told her that it was going to last all night long, it had been no idle threat. It had always been dynamite between them, even at the end, but in the past there had always been an air of him holding back, of treating her as though she were so fragile she might break. But last night there had been no holding back. He had made love to her as if he had just re-invented sex and, oh, he had taken her to heaven and back with exquisite ease—the years of abstinence had sharpened her appetite, had increased her hunger so that it equalled his.

Through her sleep-fuddled brain, some warning bell rang. *The years of abstinence.* Her eyelids flew open as she looked around in disbelief. She was not lying in the rumpled bed of a small log cabin, with verdant Italian mountains filling the windows with all their glory. Instead, she lay alone in a narrow bed. Her bed. Her flat. A silent groan escaped her lips. What had she done?

Oh, God—what hadn't she done? She'd let Stefano bring her home and make love to her.

Let him? mocked a cynical voice. She'd virtually torn his clothes from his body in her eagerness.

Her mind took in the emptiness of the space in the bed beside her. He had left her bed, and very soon he would be out of her life completely.

What had she *done*? All that work for nothing—
those days, those weeks, those months carefully trying
to erase him from her mind. All those tear-soaked pillows, which had gradually ceased, leaving her to cau-
tiously believe that one day there might be another life
for her, after Stefano. And now, with a rashness which
was unbelievable—she had thrown it all away.

She heard the tap being turned off, and hastily half
shut her eyes. Perhaps he was coming back to bed with
her... But when, minutes later, he walked quietly into
the bedroom, fully dressed, her heart sank. A cold chill
caught at her skin as she watched him knotting the
silk tie, before silently slipping his feet into the soft
leather shoes.

'I'm not asleep,' she said. 'There's no need for you
to creep around.'

He looked up, startled, and she thought that he
looked uncomfortable. 'I didn't want to wake you,' he
said, and picked up the heavy gold wristwatch. The
eyes which studied her were guarded. 'I'm afraid that
I have business to attend to.'

At this early hour? Just who did he think he was
kidding? She felt like screaming, or bursting into tears,
anything other than give herself up to the pain which
was threatening to swamp her. Now what? she wanted
to know. Why are we having this non-conversation—
pretending that last night never happened? But
wouldn't it be simply to hold up any remaining pride
and see it contemptuously smashed if she asked him
the question which was on her lips? The question
which she despised herself for even wanting to ask—
about whether they had any future together, or whether

it had just been a moment of wild weakness, of his lust and her longing—both gone out of control.

He sat down on the edge of the bed, but he kept his distance, she noted. There had not been one word nor gesture this morning to indicate that last night had been anything other than carnal desire on his part.

'About last night...' he began.

She heard the studiedly neutral tone of his voice, and her heart plummeted. She wanted the night preserved intact, so that she could remember how it had felt. On lonely nights she would allow herself to think about it. She didn't want it destroyed by his regrets. She pinned a nonchalant smile to her kiss-bruised lips. 'Let's forget it ever happened,' she said.

The dark eyes narrowed. '*Forget* it?' he echoed tightly. 'Cressida, what are you saying?'

I'm saying that I still love you, but that for you it's simply good old-fashioned lust, that's what I'm saying, she thought. 'I'm saying that it was very—nice...' She backed against the pillows as she witnessed the fury on his face.

'*Nice*?' he thundered. '*Nice*?'

'Far be it for me to cast aspersions on your sexual—prowess,' she said coolly. 'All right, it was great—you know it was, but let's not play games with one another.' And as she stared at him, she read the truth in his eyes. 'It was the reason you brought me home, wasn't it, Stefano? You got what you came for, didn't you?'

He looked at her for one cold, hard minute, before standing up. 'Yes,' he said flatly. 'I did.' And he turned and left the room, and the flat, without another word.

She stared at the door after he'd gone, as if by some magic she could bring him back again, back into her arms where everything had been all right.

But then slowly, relentlessly, the unwelcome thoughts began flooding back. Where was Stefano going now—to 'work' or, in reality, back to Ebony?

She closed her eyes in anguish as she remembered that she hadn't given Ebony a second thought last night.

How could she have sunk so low as to go to bed with her husband when he was involved with someone else? To have had so little from him, when she had once had so much?

Turning her face into the pillow, she began to cry.

CHAPTER TEN

CRESSIDA didn't leave her flat for two days, doing little other than sleeping. She had read once, somewhere, that the body often shut right down, using sleep as a refuge, protecting the mind from thoughts which were too painful to endure.

But even in her sleep she could not be free of Stefano. Images of the arrogantly handsome face came back to haunt her, mocking her, tormenting her with memories of how humiliating it felt to be loved, and left.

She awoke on the third day and decided to make an effort. She dressed in her most flattering navy and white 'audition' dress and went to see Arnie, her agent.

Arnie took one look at her and champed on his cigar in exasperation.

'Hell, Cressida!' he exclaimed. 'What have you been doing to yourself?'

She shrugged. 'I've lost a bit of weight,' she said defensively. 'So what? Lots of women do.'

'Not when they start out your size,' he contradicted, then shook his head. 'I can't send you for jobs looking like a half-starved waif. Tell you what—why don't you take a couple of weeks off? Feed yourself up, get some fresh air into your cheeks. Haven't you got an aunt who lives in the country, or somewhere?'

'Cornwall.'

'Well, can't you go and stay with her?'

She could of course, Cressida reflected as she stopped off at the supermarket on the way back to the flat. But if she'd shocked Arnie with her appearance, then she couldn't possibly go and worry her ageing aunt.

So she stayed in her flat and tried to feed herself up, but the meals she ate were burnt up by nervous energy. She felt so low that she left the phone off the hook—she couldn't face talking to anyone—and if her aunt rang and heard her dead, flat voice it would only worry the hell out of her. She felt unable to settle to anything—neither books nor television—and gradually the strain began to tell. One night, while contemplating the bleakness of her future, she found herself shivering uncontrollably.

She managed to crawl to her bed on legs in which bone had suddenly been replaced by jelly, and huddled beneath every blanket and duvet she could lay her hands on, before giving herself up to a deep and dreamless sleep.

A drum was beating somewhere—where? Distant and muffled and persistent. Cressida half opened swollen eyelids to see who had the effrontery to play the drums in her flat.

'Oh, someone's at the front door,' she croaked in surprise, registering that, although daylight was flooding through the windows, all the lights were glaring, and that the television was loudly playing her least-favourite soap opera.

'Shut up,' she croaked, as the banging persisted, and then her mouth fell open as she looked through her open bedroom door in time to see the front door bending inwards and then, with an almighty crash, it buckled and splintered right off its hinges, and Stefano, in black jeans and a black T-shirt almost fell in, his angry eyes sweeping around the flat, until he saw her and marched across to her, grabbing her by the shoulders to lever her up to face him.

'What the *hell* do you think you're playing at?' he shouted. He looked round at the loud whine of the disconnected phone and, swearing softly, he hurled it back into its cradle. 'Are you trying to kill yourself?' he demanded. 'People have been worried *sick* about you.'

'People?' she croaked. Including him?

'No one's been able to get hold of you. Adrian and Alexia have been trying to ring you for days. They saw us leave the last-night party together and thought that I might know where you were. They've left streams of messages at my office. And now I return from Italy to find you half dead. Are you *crazy*?' His fingers dug into her arms.

'You're hurting me,' she complained. 'And I'm cold.'

Narrowed eyes swept over her, taking in her clammy skin, the thick jumper she wore, the heap of duvets and blankets piled high, and with a muttered expletive he tore them off her and tossed them aside.

'Don't touch me!' she shouted, in very real alarm. She couldn't bear that, she honestly couldn't bear that.

Even in her befuddled state she knew that she would rather have nothing of him than the odd scrap of himself he was prepared to give her.

His mouth twisted, but only fleetingly. 'Do you think I am reduced to taking advantage of sick women?' he said bitterly, and then his voice unexpectedly softened. 'And now the sweater, *cara*, will have to come off.'

She registered that he was systematically divesting her of her jumper and her ski-pants in the most asexual way possible, before laying her back against the pillows.

And then it all became a blur—Stefano talking in rapid Italian on the telephone—Stefano shouting at her—ordering her to drink, and it seemed like forever before he would let her obey her aching eyelids and fall asleep against something both soft and strong, something which felt much too comfortably like Stefano's chest.

CHAPTER ELEVEN

CRESSIDA awoke to an ever present, familiar drone and the realisation that she felt dreadful. It was several minutes before she felt like opening her eyes to stare round her in growing disbelief. She was on a plane! Her eyelids fluttered. And not an ordinary plane either—it was the private jet which Stefano sometimes leased. What the hell was going on? She turned her head with difficulty to find him sitting beside her, surprising a look of concern on the normally harsh features.

He stared down at the huge eyes in the white face. 'So you are awake at last,' he observed.

A strange muzziness filled her head. Her words sounded weighted, and odd. 'What's been happening? Where are you taking me?' she demanded.

Stefano pressed a bell at his side, and, when a doe-eyed stewardess appeared, ordered coffee and mineral water in rapid Italian.

'Drink some water first,' he ordered. 'You have been very sick.'

'Sick?' Shakily she drank some of the water he offered her, feeling her strength return as she did so.

'Where are you taking me?' she repeated.

'To Italy. To my villa.'

She stared at him in bewilderment.

'You need to recuperate, and you certainly won't be able to recuperate in that flat,' he continued calmly. 'There is no one to look after you and,' he paused for a moment, 'like it or not—you are my responsibility.'

'My responsibility'. How onerous he made those words sound. And what a humiliating reason for bringing her here. And Ebony—what of her? Cressida shuddered at the very real possibility that Ebony might already be installed at his villa. But surely even Stefano would not flaunt his indiscretion in such a way?

He must have seen her reaction, for he leaned forward, his words very measured. 'Listen to me. You have no job. You have been very sick. You are exhausted, and you haven't been eating properly. When I returned from my business trip and found you at your flat—you were in a terrible state. And if I had not...' He shook his head. 'Do you not realise? You looked half dead!'

'And why should you care?' she asked bitterly.

'I care,' he said slowly, and in spite of everything her schoolgirl heart leapt. 'Because you might be pregnant with my child.

She turned stunned and frightened green eyes on him. 'No,' she whispered. 'I can't be. I thought that you—'

He looked at her with barely concealed impatience. '*Cristo*!' he swore. 'You are a married woman, not a child. Yes, I used something—but not that first time. That time I lost my head. You were too—' He paused deliberately. 'Frantic for it, my love.'

She buried her face in her hands, the enormity of what he'd said hitting her like a lead weight. 'Oh, my

God,' she said in a strangled whisper, and then looked up to meet his eyes. 'What if I am?'

His face was completely imperturbable. 'We will cross that bridge if and when we get to it. It might never happen. Come, *cara*—drink your coffee. We acted together and we must face the consequences together. I am offering to take care of you until we know for sure.'

And a small sigh of relief escaped her, for she now honestly doubted whether Ebony would be around. She might be an understanding mistress, but Cressida doubted whether she would be able to stomach finding out whether or not Stefano had made his wife pregnant. She tried to sit up, and failed. 'How did I get here?'

'You were virtually unconscious when the doctor arrived,' he said, matter-of-factly. 'I had you taken to my hotel suite, where you were diagnosed as having a severe viral infection. My doctor recommended complete rest, and that is what I intend you shall have. He also gave you a light sedative.'

'You've had me drugged,' she interjected, her voice tinged with hysteria.

He ignored the interruption as if she hadn't spoken. 'Getting hold of your passport was not a problem,' he said. 'And I decided that we should leave for Italy without further delay. You look awful,' he finished with characteristic candour.

But his words scarcely registered; her mind was frantically trying to work out dates, wondering if she could possibly be, as he had suggested—pregnant. What had Stefano said? 'We will cross that bridge if and when we get to it. It might never happen.'

Or it just might. He might be able to dismiss it lightly. She was not able to do the same. Not when— the thought was one of desperation—not when his child might now be growing inside her womb. Without her realising that she did it, her pale hand reached down and instinctively rested on the flat line of her belly.

It was all like some bizarre dream, she thought. What if she was pregnant? What if she *was*? She stole a glance at Stefano, who was now engrossed in paperwork, his black-inked gold pen decisively circling words and scoring whole sentences out.

What on earth would she do? Because even if she *was* pregnant—Stefano didn't want her. He had Ebony now.

The plane landed and they were whisked through Customs and Immigration to be shown to a limousine parked directly outside the terminal, a sister car to the one he had in London, in Paris, and New York. She sat in the back seat with him, glancing at him apprehensively.

'This is madness,' she told him. 'Sheer and utter madness.'

He shrugged, with a small movement of the broad, linen-covered shoulders. 'So what? It's good to be crazy once in a while. Relax. Enjoy the scenery.'

The countryside sped by, but she stared at it sightlessly, and the purr of the powerful engine was strangely soothing so that, presently, she slept.

'Cressida…' A soft, deep voice came to her as if from a great distance, and Cressida came to slowly, waking up to find that she was somehow cradled up next to Stefano, her head had slipped on to his chest, and her first sensations on waking were having her nostrils filled with his heady masculine scent, her cheek rubbed by the silkily fine substance of his shirt.

'We're here.'

'Yes.' She moved away from him and stretched, away from the tantalising proximity of the strong, hard body, blinking a little in the sunshine as she stepped out of the car, her first sight of the villa sending a pang through her. She had never been happy here. They had come to this house every weekend of their short-lived marriage, to be surrounded by family and servants—every moment of their time caught up in the frenetic round of social activities which Stefano's high-born relatives delighted in. At times she had felt that the only time she saw Stefano was in bed, and at least there she had thought that she could compensate for her poor attempts at partnering him at the dinner table—the overwhelmed young foreign girl. But even in bed, she had been full of youthful insecurities—and when the pleasure he gave her had faded, she would lie awake, comparing her shyness with the sophisticated experience of the other women he had known...

'Cressida,' Stefano's voice urged her back to the present, 'Rosa is waiting.'

The reality of seeing Rosa, the housekeeper, and Luciano her husband, gardener and odd-job man, suddenly filled her with an inexplicable feeling of dread, and she stared up at Stefano. 'What on earth are we going to tell them?'

His mouth curled very slightly and, in that moment, he was very much the Italian aristocrat.

'It is not for you to have to explain your actions to

the servants,' he said arrogantly. 'You are mistress of this house.'

Her green eyes widened. Madness, she had thought in the car, but Stefano's madness was, it seemed, a little more than temporary. 'But I'm not—'

He took her by the shoulders and looked down at her. 'While you are here, at least—you are mistress of my house.'

'While you are here'. The words mocked her, throwing in her face the brevity of her tenure, and the weepiness which had threatened to swamp her since she'd woken up made her knees sag beneath her, and she heard him swear, before scooping her up into his arms as if she were so many feathers.

Her eyelids fluttered over her eyes, afraid that he might see through to how appallingly wonderful it felt to be carried like this by him, and with a pang she was reminded of when he had brought her here after their honeymoon—had carried her over this same threshold. But then his face had been full of laughter, nothing like the stern-featured man who now carried her. It shouldn't feel like this, she thought desperately. Let me feel nothing in his arms. 'Don't,' she whispered. 'Put me down.'

'You would prefer to walk, perhaps to collapse again?' he asked tightly, but he didn't put her down, carrying her to the cool white room which overlooked the gardens. 'Rosa will help you undress,' he told her. 'Then you must rest.'

She stared up at him, determined to fight him all the way, even though she had all the strength of a newly born kitten. 'I don't want to—'

'Rest,' he ordered, with an air which brooked no

argument, and deposited her in the centre of the large
bed, leaving her staring helplessly at his retreating
back as he strode from the room.

That evening, she remembered Rosa brushing the
long red hair with tender care as though she had been
a child. But mostly she slept—a deep, dreamless sleep
where even Stefano couldn't haunt her. And some
time—it must have been during the night, she
thought—she woke to find Stefano standing over her,
watching her, an indescribable expression on his face.
Almost…surely not *tenderness*? No, she knew that she
must have dreamt *that*, for the following morning she
awoke to find him beside her bed, the familiar sardonic
expression in place again.

Aware of the filmy lace nightgown which Rosa had
given her, and of the bare flesh which it exposed, she
felt colour wash over her cheekbones. 'What is it?'
she asked him.

'You have slept very late, Cressida, and the doctor
has arrived. He wishes to examine you.' The doctor
came, asking Cressida swiftly assessing questions, and
Stefano hovered in the background, readjusting the
straps of her nightgown for her after the examination.
She felt his hands brush against her breasts and a
tremor ran through her. She saw the dark eyes narrow
in comprehension, and she lay back against the pillows, hating her betraying response to him. For hadn't
it been that which had got her into this whole mess in
the first place?

'As you have been told, it is stress,' announced the
doctor. 'But she is young, my friend. Rest cures a great
many ills.'

The dark eyes glittered as he addressed the doctor.

'While you are here, you might like to know that my wife,' Stefano's voice sounded strangely husky, but his eyes dared her to challenge his use of the title, 'might be with child.'

'Indeed?' The doctor gave a small exclamation of pleasure.

'And when do you expect your period, Signora di Camilla?'

Again Cressida blushed. How horrified the doctor would be if he knew of the circumstances surrounding her possible pregnancy. 'On the seventeenth.'

'And it is regular?'

'As clockwork.'

'So when can we expect to know?' asked Stefano impatiently.

He can't wait to get rid of me, she recognised, and leant her head back into the pillow. The doctor smiled. 'With the sophisticated testing methods available nowadays, it is possible to know immediately. I would say in seven days hence. You must be very happy, Stefano.'

'No confirmation has been given, and speculation serves little use,' said Stefano abruptly.

She lay back on the pillows, recognising that he had neatly side-stepped the doctor's question. Happy? How could he be happy if she was pregnant? He would see it as a constricting trap.

She waited until he came back after seeing the doctor out. 'You must be praying like mad,' she said slowly.

The dark eyes glittered down at her. 'For what?'

'That I'm not—pregnant.' In a dream-world he would deny her accusation vehemently. But this was the real world, and he did not. 'It would be a disaster for you wouldn't it? What would you do?' And how on earth would you break it to Ebony?

He turned his back to her and stood staring out at the tall blue cypress trees in the distance. 'I would take the most expedient course of action, Cressida,' he said carefully, and then, as if not wanting to continue, changed the subject completely. 'You may come down for dinner tonight. The physician assures me that you are now well rested.'

She looked over at him as he stood beside the window, his hands in his trousers pockets, stretching the fine material across the muscular thighs. Outwardly, he looked relaxed, but always, with Stefano, there was that underlying air of watchfulness and tension. Yes, she thought, he would take the most expedient course of action—he would always make the best of whatever fate threw at him. But what about her? Was she just an expedient to him?

The dark eyes were glittering in question. 'But perhaps you wish to have supper here? A tray in your room?'

If she had an ounce of sense she would say yes, and stay away from him. His presence was painfully poignant, and yet she found herself pulled by the magnetism of the man, like some helpless addict.

'What time is dinner?' she asked.

'At eight.'

'I'll be down.'

She slept until seven, then showered and dressed in preparation for the meal.

There was a knock on the door, and she hastily pulled her wrap around her, not wanting Stefano to

see her in the flimsy items of lingerie, see the light
grow in his eyes and issue a challenge which she
might not be able to resist.

But it was not Stefano, but Rosa, who stood at the
door with her friendly smile. She spoke in faltering
English.

'Signor di Camilla says that you will find something
to wear for dinner in the wardrobe.' She gestured with
a careworn hand. 'Would you like that I help you to
dress?'

Cressida shook her head. What clothes? She had
come with only the clothes she had been wearing;
she'd assumed that she would wear those. The night-
dress she had worn had been new. 'I can manage perfectly, thank you, Rosa,' she told her, waiting until the
door had closed behind the housekeeper before she
pulled open the wardrobe door to find, to her astonishment, that every beautiful and costly item of cloth-
ing she had ever owned during her marriage was hanging in shrouds of protective plastic. Wonderingly, her
fingers touched a black velvet, a kingfisher silk with
beaded bodice, row upon row of cashmere, silk and
pure Swiss lace. Even the underwear, the night-
clothes—wisps of gossamer-fine drifts lay in palest
colour co-ordinated piles. He had kept them all here,
but why? When she had left, on that bright summer
day when even the fierce heat had been unable to
warm her chilled skin, she had forsworn everything he
had ever bought her, determined to take with her nothing of his.

She sank down on to the bed, momentarily confused, and more than a little shaken. It was a strange
feeling, looking at these symbols of a former life. A

whole wardrobe, completely intact—almost as though they were lying…in *wait*? No, surely not. She shook her head, as if to clear it, then set about choosing something to wear for dinner. She deliberately avoided the snowy organza gown, and the black lace. He had loved her in both those dresses, and whenever she had worn them… She bit her lip, willing the thoughts to go. If she allowed herself to wander back down memory lane, then she would be lost.

In the end, she chose a short emerald silk which echoed the green of her eyes. The thick hair she twisted up into a top-knot, and slowly walked down to dinner.

He was standing on the terrace with his back to her, wearing the snowy white dinner-jacket which suited him so well. The night was warm enough, with a moon the size of a dinner plate which spilled its silver light on to his dark hair. He heard her and turned round slowly, his eyes briefly running from the top of her gleaming red hair to the tips of her emerald-shoed toes, her legs slimly pale in the silk stockings she'd chosen.

'You look very beautiful,' he said, at last.

She shook her head. 'Don't, Stefano. If beauty it is, then it's been nothing but a curse to me.'

The dark eyes were curious. 'Oh?' he drawled. 'You intrigue me, Cressida. And I can't believe for a moment that what you say is true.'

'Isn't it?' Unable to bear the inquisitive searching of his eyes, she turned to stare at the moon. 'Beauty's a very transient attribute. And the reason you fell in love with me.' She faced him once more. 'Shall I tell you something? It makes a woman feel pretty insecure to feel she's loved for her beauty alone. The opposite to an antique, in fact, because as time goes on, and her looks fade, she becomes less valuable, instead of more.'

The dark eyes had narrowed, and he shook his head in contradiction. 'I can't deny that your beauty attracted me, but what I fell in love with was what lay beneath—your spirit, your enthusiasm. You were that beguiling combination of innocence with a smouldering sensuality which lay just beneath the surface. Ice with fire. It was quite—irresistible.' He smiled. 'As was your complete uninterest in my wealth. It was,' he said, with a quiet cynicism, 'amazingly enough— it was the first time in my life that I felt that a woman wanted *me*, and not what I represented.' His mouth turned down at the corners. 'Most of your sex are dazzled by glitter, Cressida, but not you. So you see— your looks were just the icing on the cake.'

It was the first time he had ever given her any indication of just what her appeal to him had been. He had never even told her that. The burden of his responsibility to the rest of his family had turned Stefano into the stereotypical 'strong and silent' type of man, a man not used to analysing his feelings. And now he had, and it was too late. With a feeling of unbearable sadness, she acknowledged the wry way he now described it, and the past tense that he used. She bit her lip to stop it trembling, searching for something to do with hands that felt clammy and redundantly out of place.

'May I have a drink, please?' she asked.

'But of course.' The broad shoulders gave the slightest of deferential shrugs. 'Forgive me. I am forgetting myself. What can I get you?' And he turned towards the drinks cabinet just inside the room.

With her question, the intimacy evaporated immediately, and she instinctively felt that there would be no more confidences from Stefano. His urbane remark concerning her choice of drinks made that perfectly clear and she found herself hating it, this new uneasy formality. She would rather be battling with him, her fists on his chest, or her words trying to wound, anything to get some kind of reaction other than this old-world politeness, as if she were some dinner guest he'd met only minutes earlier.

'Just some juice would be fine,' she managed, matching his formal tone with his own.

He nodded, tipping some of her favourite papaya juice into a long crystal beaker together with crushed ice. She took it from him, her hand mercifully steady, staring into the handsome face.

'Shall we sit?' He pointed to a small sofa, but she shook her head.

At least standing she felt less vulnerable. If he had her next to him on a small sofa, who knew how she might react? Because she found herself wanting to be held by him, to be close to him as she had been that night at her flat, while he stood watching her, as impenetrable as a statue.

'You kept all my clothes,' she observed, her eyes searching his face.

'You sound surprised.'

She swallowed. 'I was. Why did you do that?'

Another shrug of the broad shoulders. 'I assumed that you would come back.'

'Come back?' Her voice was tremulous.

'Naturally, I thought that you would be back, if for nothing else than to collect what amounted to a large wardrobe which you would inevitably have difficulty in replacing.' His mouth tightened with irritation. 'It did not occur to me that you would be so stubborn as to make no effort to claim them.'

Light flared in her green eyes. 'I wanted to start anew.'

'Ah!'

His sardonic tone lit a fuse. 'Yes, anew! Afresh! And those clothes would never have suited the kind of life I intended to lead.'

'Evidently not,' he retorted. 'Sackcloth might have been better, judging from what I saw of your lifestyle.'

She had been wrong in wanting some reaction, any reaction. The fighting hurt as much now as it had ever hurt. 'I wanted to taste independence,' she said in a small voice in one last-ditch attempt to explain to him how lost and alone she had felt. 'The independence you had promised me, and then denied me.'

'But independence is not to be given, Cressida,' he said softly. 'It is to be taken.'

'How could I take it when you dominated me completely!' she accused.

'Then why did you let me,' he queried. 'Mmm?'

Because you were strong and I was weak, she thought sadly. I was in awe of your worldliness. She put the papaya juice down on to a small table. 'This isn't going to work, my staying here—we both know that, Stefano.'

'On the contrary,' he said smoothly. 'I know nothing of the sort. And now is neither the time nor the place to discuss it. You are still weak, and only just out of bed, and Rosa is waiting to serve us dinner. And,' his face was momentarily serious, 'you must eat, and recover. It is imperative that you take care of yourself.'

And, of course, his child, if a child there was. The implication was very clear. Cressida suddenly got a good idea of how he would cosset and protect her if that were to be the case.

'We're dining alone?' she asked, somehow expecting a member of his family to be in evidence, as they so often were.

His eyes glinted. 'We are. Completely.'

During dinner Stefano set out to be at his most charming, and yet Cressida found the false intimacy far too poignant to be relaxing and in spite of Rosa's delicious food she did little more than push the food around her plate. And when they took coffee in the sitting-room, she steeled herself, watching as he dropped a small cube of sugar into her coffee unasked. 'Do you honestly think that we can live here amicably for the next week?'

'I believe we can try. You see—I told you once before, Cressida—I will take the most expedient course of action.'

It was certainly not the answer which her foolish heart hoped for, but perhaps it was the best she could hope for in the circumstances.

He was looking at her closely. 'And tomorrow,' he told her, 'we will take a drive into the hills.'

'You aren't working?' she asked in surprise.

He eyed her closely. 'Not tomorrow. And now, I think, I must send you to bed. You are weary, yes?'

Not a single attempt to touch her. Even that had

died. She nodded, not trusting herself to speak, and in her room she tiredly changed into her nightgown. But as she pulled the door to, she heard Stefano's deep voice talking softly into the phone. To Ebony, no doubt. Counting the days until they could be together again.

And then she really *was* weary—too weary to do anything other than drag herself over to her bed, and to collapse under the soft, snowy sheets.

CHAPTER TWELVE

To HER surprise, Cressida slept deeply, but when conscious thought invaded her on awaking she remembered Stefano's late-night phone call once he had got rid of her to her room. And she had agreed to drive with him into the mountains today!

Alone with him in the intimate atmosphere of a car. Susceptible to the powerful aura of the man. It was sheer madness to accompany him, but what was the alternative? To spend long days here with him at the villa, was that not equally claustrophobic?

She looked out of the window. And it was *such* a glorious day, one of the most beautiful kinds of day that Italy could offer—with the light, warm breeze causing the filmy material of the curtains to billow into soft clouds around her window. She made up her mind in an instant as she swung her legs over the side of the bed. She would go. She would play her part. But she would give no indication of her true feelings for Stefano, and there would be no more physical intimacy. For that way lay heartbreak.

The dining-room was empty, and Rosa brought her warm bread, fresh figs and juice, watching with an expression of satisfaction as Cressida tucked in hungrily.

'It is good?' she asked.

'It's very good!' smiled Cressida, recognising the genuine affection in the housekeeper's eyes. Had she ever really felt intimidated by this friendly and fiercely loyal woman? Or had it just been the idea of servants in general which she had found so hard to come to terms with? She had had none of Stefano's easy familiarity with Rosa and her husband and her fumbling attempts to find a happy ground on which to communicate with them had battered her confidence still further. She had convinced herself that they had disapproved of her, had wanted Stefano to marry an Italian woman of similar class—but could she now accept that perhaps she had imagined censure where none existed? 'You've been very kind to me, Rosa,' she said quietly. 'Looked after me like a mother when I was ill.'

The Italian woman shook her head. 'You no trouble when you're ill, *signora*—the *signore* now, *he* trouble!'

As Rosa left the room, Cressida could hear her talking in rapid Italian which was impossible for her to understand.

Wiping her mouth with her napkin, Cressida looked up to find Stefano watching her, the dark, unreadable eyes flicking over the slender length of her body where the crisp white cotton dress moulded the small high bust and the tan leather belt accentuated her slim waist. He was also dressed informally—with an open-necked white shirt tucked into belted grey linen trousers.

'Good morning,' he smiled. 'Rosa tells me that you're eating again.'

The solicitous expression in his eyes meant nothing

other than courtesy, she reminded herself. 'Rosa's cooking is so good,' she replied, 'that only a fool would refuse it.'

'But you never eat when you're unhappy, do you? Like last night?' he persisted. 'So may I take your hunger as a good omen?'

With a trace of amusement lighting the dark eyes, he looked like a god standing there, she thought. A god who no longer loved her, who had declared nothing but his desire. In her own best interests it was imperative she stay impervious to the charm which he had in so much abundance when he cared to exercise it. She pushed the chair back and stood up. 'You may interpret it as you see fit,' she said neutrally, making as if to move past him, but a light hand on her bare arm stopped her with a movement which, infuriatingly, sent her pulses racing.

'Cressida,' he said softly. 'Today we have a holiday. Today we don't fight. OK?'

She stared into eyes which were at at their most persuasive. Fighting was tiring, it was true, but at least you could hide your true feelings behind harsh words. Without those, what might she betray?

'OK?' The brown eyes were almost soft, the voice cajoling. 'A—how do you say?—truce?'

Cressida laughed. 'Oh, all right,' she agreed. 'You know very well it's what we say. And you can stop batting your eyelashes at me now.'

His answering laugh rang out, rich and velvety, and Cressida realised how rarely she had heard it these past weeks. 'I'll get my jacket,' she said quickly.

'I'll wait in the car.'

Minutes later she had buckled herself in beside him and the gun-metal-grey sports car roared away.

'Where are you taking me?' she asked.

'You'll see,' he answered non-committally. 'Relax.'

She tried, forcing her mind to concentrate on the scenery, resolutely trying to ignore the imposing presence of the man. And the drive *was* relaxing, accompanied as it was by his favourite Vivaldi, filling the air with soft, sweet notes.

He took her to a restaurant she'd never visited before—with vast windows overlooking the hills which artists had been replicating for centuries. Neutral territory, she thought, and their conversation was suitably neutral, for they conversed like polite strangers.

'You like it?' he enquired urbanely.

She nodded, searching for a tone which was equally casual. 'It's new?'

'Fairly. I discovered it a few months ago. It was opened by an old schoolfriend of mine. Do you remember he used to have the Casa Romana?'

Their favourite restaurant. Of course she remembered. Did he really think she could have forgotten? 'Yes, I remember,' she said dully.

And of course he had been leading his own life during their separation, discovering restaurants, going to films, theatre trips, holidays—logically she knew all that. And yet it hurt like hell to think of his carrying on without her. Was that because he had succeeded in adapting to their separation, while it was patently obvious that she had failed?

'Would you like some coffee?' he asked, at the end of the meal.

She wanted to bang her fists on the table, uncaring

of what their fellow diners thought. How could he sit there making polite conversation as though they were two normal people out enjoying a meal together? As though there weren't this fundamental question burning away at the forefronts of their minds—about whether or not she was pregnant, and what they were going to do about it if she was.

But Stefano was sitting there, oblivious to her inner turmoil, one eyebrow laconically raised. 'Some coffee?' he prompted again.

'Please.'

'I'm going to have to be at the office tomorrow,' he told her in the car on the way home. 'But you should find plenty to amuse yourself. Spend your days reading by the pool, mmm?'

'Or shopping?' she tested. 'May I have the car?'

There was a discernible glint as he glanced at her. 'Any shopping you require, we'll do together, I think.'

'You think I'll run away to England?' she hazarded. 'But there's nothing to stop me doing that while you're working, is there?'

'Not without your passport,' he remarked urbanely.

'So I really *am* your prisoner!' she accused.

'Not at all,' he corrected softly. 'It's all a question of perception, Cressida. I prefer to think of it as "guest".'

'Prisoner.'

But he was right and she was wrong; it didn't feel in the least like prison. She relaxed into the luxurious surroundings like a cat who had found the sun after months in darkness. She slept late, and ate huge breakfasts, taking her book and her hat out to lie on one of the loungers beside the pool. She had found all her old swimwear—including one favourite silky white draped one-piece.

It was a dream world, not a real world—one where she let reality retreat, where she suspended belief, and forgot why she was really here. And bizarrely it became how their marriage should have been, but never was. She was no longer champing at the bit to go out to work in an effort to prove herself, or constantly worrying about what people thought of her. Indolent and replete as she felt the good food, the fresh air and the swimming mend her body, she began to look forward to Stefano returning from the office in the evening.

Until she pulled herself up to remind herself that the reason for the dream-like quality of her existence was because it was exactly that. It was borrowed time she was living on. This was *his* world, not hers. His and Ebony's. She must never forget the reasons for her being here—a rash moment which could have momentous repercussions. And Stefano's concern for her was simply because he always wanted to do the 'right' thing. She was still his wife, and, as long as that remained the case, he still considered her his responsibility.

One afternoon, she dozed off by the pool. She had barely slept a wink the night before, because the period she had convinced herself would arrive that day had not done so. She awoke with a start and glanced at her watch to see that it was almost five. Time for a quick swim before getting ready for dinner, she thought, standing up to stretch at the side of the pool, realising how much she would miss her life here as she surveyed the sparkling turquoise depths.

Her bikini was brief—two cleverly cut fragments of jade silk, and she closed her eyes, raised her hands above her head and dived her way into the water like an arrow. The cool water made her gasp, and she swam several lengths before turning to float on her back, her hair fanning out in the water behind her, when she felt the warmth of the sun blotted out, and she opened her eyes quickly to find Stefano standing there, dressed in one of his darkly elegant office suits.

She felt suddenly and ridiculously vulnerable as she stared up at him.

'That looks very inviting,' he said lightly, his eyes moving to the swell of her breasts, the line of her nipples clear beneath the soaking fabric. 'I think I'll join you.'

She swallowed. 'I—I'm just getting out,' she stammered.

'Well, don't,' he said. 'Wait for me.' And he turned and headed for the small changing cabin.

She licked the chlorine-flavoured water off her lips nervously. Of course she didn't have to wait for him. Nothing was stopping her from pulling herself out of the water and going back into the house. So why did she stay right where she was?

And then it *was* too late, Stefano had removed his clothes in double quick time and had donned some dark, low briefs which left very little to the imagination. She felt her pulse begin to hammer as her eyes travelled over the broad torso, at the rock hard thighs with their sprinkling of hair. At...

Oh, God! She couldn't do it. If she stayed in the water with him...

As he dived into the pool, she hauled herself out,

hurriedly enveloping herself in the thick towelling
robe, pushing wet hair back off her face to find that
he had surfaced, water streaming down the smooth
olive skin, and was watching her—mocking amusement in the dark eyes.

'Going so soon?' he taunted softly.

'I have to change for dinner.'

'Do you now?'

The deep voice sounded so ridiculously...*erotic* that
colour flared in her cheeks as she bent to pick up her
book with a shaking hand.

'Cressida?'

She stared at him. 'What?'

'You're...' He hesitated. 'All right?'

She knew exactly what he meant, and her thoughts
on borrowed time came rushing back to torment her.
'Well, I haven't found out if I'm pregnant yet, if that's
what you're getting at,' she snapped.

He ignored her outburst, just continued to survey
her. 'Oh, by the way,' he said casually, 'we've been
invited to a dinner. On Saturday. My mother and my
sister will be there. It's at the di Tomasis' house.'

His eyes were assessing her reaction and she took
up the challenge. Yes, she *had* disliked the cloyingly
formal dinners, had felt like a freak on show in front
of his sophisticated friends, but now some element of
pride prompted her to redeem herself, to show them
all that she was no longer the little foreigner, cowed
by them all.

'They know I'm here?'

'Naturally.'

'And what have you told them?'

'I am not required to provide explanations about my

personal life to my family. They know nothing of your reasons for being here.'

'In that case, I'll come with you on Saturday.'

She had expected surprise, but there was none. Instead he nodded. 'Good.' And he dived beneath the water again.

The di Tomasis family were old friends of the di Camillas—an older couple with grown-up children of their own.

Cressida and Stefano drove up outside the floodlit mansion, and, judging by the number of cars parked outside, they were among the last to arrive, Cressida decided, as she glanced around surreptitiously for any sign of Stefano's family. She let Stefano open the passenger door of the car for her, the roof up despite the warm night in deference, she assumed, to her hair, which she had piled up into a complicated top-knot. It made her look older, and she knew it; she suspected that was why she had done it, and that her dress had been chosen for exactly the same reason. In draped violet voile, it was ageless and utterly classic. Cressida knew that on the outside she looked the epitome of cool sophistication, but inside her stomach was churning as she faced the prospect of renewing her uneasy relationship with her in-laws.

But her reunion with Stefano's mother was entirely unexpected, and she had to hide her shock as she looked at the older woman. In two years she had aged dramatically. To Cressida, despite the still fine dark eyes and the aristocratic bearing, she appeared so much smaller than she remembered. And it seemed to Cressida that she greeted her with far more warmth than she had ever shown during her marriage, or was that simply wishful thinking?

And yet it was the same with Gina, Stefano's sister, there with Angelo, her husband. At the time of their marriage, she had made little secret of the fact that she considered Cressida unsuitable, particularly as she had done her best to match-make for one of her schoolfriends and her brother. But now she stepped forward, her beautiful face wreathed in smiles, to exchange the familiar two kisses on either cheek.

'Cressida,' she said warmly. 'You look wonderful.' And Cressida saw her meet her brother's eyes with a nod.

'So do you,' said Cressida. 'Absolutely glowing.'

'Ah!' Gina's face was conspiratorial. 'I hope so— for there is a reason for that. Shall I tell them, *caro*?' She flashed dark eyes, so similar to Stefano's, at her husband, who grinned and raised his eyebrows.

'I guess you're going to anyway,' he remarked.

'I'm going to have a baby!' beamed Gina. 'I'm pregnant!'

Faint colour washed at Cressida's cheekbones as congratulations echoed around the room, and she met Stefano's searching gaze, but she looked away, terrified that he would discover what she wanted above all else.

And then she saw the proud look in Angelo's eyes and a feeling of immense sadness came over her. For even if she *was* pregnant, she would never inspire that look of protective, paternal pride in Stefano's eyes.

There were eight to dinner in the chandeliered salon—the di Tomasis themselves, Gina and Angelo, Stefano's mother, and Filipo—one of the di Tomasis' sons at home for the weekend from college. Cressida was seated opposite Stefano and next to his mother.

She was aware of two things: of a definite thawing in the attitude of his mother towards her—she had not imagined it—and of Stefano listening to every word they spoke, even while nodding and joining in the general conversation around the table. She knew that he was listening, she could read it in every line of his body. She wondered if he was policing her conversation, afraid that she might blurt something out.

But it was after the dinner was finished that she was most surprised, when Gina followed her from the room.

'Come and sit with me and we'll drink coffee,' she said, linking her arm through Cressida's.

They walked through to the formal salon, where tiny cups of strong coffee were being served. Cressida prepared herself for an interrogation, but the discussion started off innocuously enough.

'Stefano tells me that you have been resting at the villa after your illness,' Gina commented.

'Resting in *both* senses of the word,' said Cressida.

Gina shook her head as she was offered coffee. 'Oh?'

'Well, it's slang for when an actor is out of work—and, as I have no job just now, that's certainly true. But yes, I have been ill.'

'And you are now better?'

'Nearly,' she prevaricated.

'And your career? Apart from this—resting—it goes well, does it not? Stefano always follows your progress, I know.'

'He *does*?' asked Cressida incredulously and then

looked up to find him standing beside her, frowning down at her from narrowed eyes.

'Cressida—I think it's time we were going,' he said in the familiarly deep voice. 'It's your first time out, and you don't want to tire yourself.'

She agreed, willingly, glad to be away from Gina's curious eyes, afraid that she might say something to give herself away. They said their farewells, and as they walked out to the car she wondered what on earth Stefano's fiercely possessive family must be making of her reappearance in his life.

She spoke to him once they were in the car. 'None of them asked me about why I was back.'

Long tanned fingers flicked the ignition key. 'My family no longer concern themselves quite so *assiduously* in my affairs,' he remarked. 'The reason that none of them asked you why you were back was because they knew it would not please me.'

She couldn't stop herself. 'And why should that be? Would they be appalled if they knew the real reason?'

He pressed on the powerful accelerator. 'It's late,' he said. 'I'm tired, and you must be, also.'

Which meant that he had no intention of discussing it, she thought, as she leaned back in the leather seat. And Stefano was a past master at blocking discussions which did not please him. He had probably shown his family the famous icy composure, which would have dared any of them to try and dig deeper into the calamitous circumstances for her being back in his life.

But when they drew up at the villa, he turned to her. 'It is, however, time for us to discuss how things stand.' There was a pause. 'Tomorrow's Sunday and

I have to go up to the cabin to check up on a few things. You may as well come along.'

She had to steel herself not to tense at the casual query—the throwaway suggestion—hurt by his attitude of playing host to a place she had always thought of as theirs. He was extending an invitation, *inviting* her to *their* cabin, their honeymoon refuge which she'd always considered somehow inviolate and unaffected by all their marital disharmony. But it would seem that she had been wrong.

And she must go with him tomorrow. It would be painful, yes, but necessary. For surely, if anything would convince her that what they once had was completely finished, it would be going there—accompanying him as some sort of guest—to see the last one of her dreams destroyed.

She forced the same airy response into her own voice. 'OK. I'll come,' she said, and without waiting for him to do it, she pushed open the car door and went into the villa without another word.

CHAPTER THIRTEEN

A FAINT breeze stirred and whispered. It was the only sound Cressida could hear in this most silent of places—on top of the mountain.

She stood for a moment staring at the small and simply built wooden building which they had reached after the gun-metal-grey sports car had ascended the impossibly narrow roads, past mountain goats which stared at them with vacant curiosity as they slowly munched at the vegetation.

The cabin.

The place where he had brought her for their honeymoon. Where he had taught her to love him. Where for three of the most wonderful weeks of her life they had lived and breathed each other, not seeing another soul and not needing anyone, save each other.

The wind, a stronger gust now, whipped the long dark red strands around her face and she turned to Stefano; his expression was unreadable, the dark glittering eyes giving nothing away.

He was unlocking the door, the key turning surprisingly easily, and then he pushed it open with a creaking sound, his arm indicating that she should precede him.

Her first surprise was that it looked so—habitable. She didn't know what she had been expecting, perhaps something like a scene from *Great Expectations*—the cabin exactly as they'd left it on that final day, but by now having thick cobwebs shrouding the tables and chairs and festooning the ceilings and walls.

He was looking down at her, his dark eyebrows drawn together in a question. 'What?'

'Someone's been coming here!'

It was as though something in her response had made him relax. The taut shoulders unbunched, the eyes narrowing briefly in humour. 'Yes, indeed—and it's not the three bears.'

She looked round, at the cups and plates and pans all neatly stacked and shining; the chairs pushed neatly underneath the table. Through the open door of the one small room which housed both seating and kitchen apparatus, she could see the wide bed, all made up, with crisp white sheets and piles of soft plaid blankets. That bed… She quickly turned her head away.

'Who?' she asked. 'You?' And Ebony too? she wondered.

He nodded. 'Sure. Every weekend I can.'

Her eyes widened automatically, finding it hard to reconcile the image of Stefano, successful and powerful businessman as he was, coming here as often as he could. A honeymoon was one thing, but she had thought that had been a one-off. She had loved the strong, practical, sensual streak he had revealed to her here, loved the man beneath all the trappings of his power and his wealth, a man unfettered by his responsibilities and employees. That man had existed only here, she had glimpsed him briefly, and yet she now discovered that this cabin had been his regular sanctuary. Who had he brought with him?

Pain invaded her system with a fierce stab as she recognised how his life had run on without her. 'What did you have to do here?' she asked dully.

His eyes were intent. 'Just check the water. The gas.' He bent to inspect a pipe beneath the sink. 'We've had some leakage lately.'

'*We've*'. She swallowed. 'I'll wait outside until you're finished.'

'As you wish.'

She wandered over to the wooden bench he'd erected in a position which had stunning views over the whole valley, but even this was unbearably poignant—she remembered how they'd sit, watching the sun sink down below the horizon and a chill would tinge the air, forcing them inside, wanting supper, but wanting each other more. Remembered long evenings playing backgammon or chess. Remembered once, too, when, soft and torpid after wine with lunch, they'd made love on that very bench... She stood up quickly, to the scent of fresh coffee drifting out on the morning air, to find Stefano in the doorway.

'I've made us coffee.'

She shook her head. The memories were like arrows piercing her. 'I'd rather get back, if you don't mind.'

'Well, I do. I told you we needed to talk.'

'Why here?'

'Why not?'

'Because...' But what could she tell him that wasn't a complete giveaway?

'Let's just say, Cressida, that up here you're my captive audience, so to speak. You can't run away. There are no servants to overhear us. Completely—

alone,' he mocked, and something in his eyes made her shake her head in denial.

'If you think—'

He shook his head impatiently. 'I haven't brought you up here to make love to you.' His eyes glinted. 'Not specifically, anyway. It's time that we touched on a few subjects we've been doing our damnedest to avoid.'

It seemed strange to hear the Americanism on his lips, but of course he had spent time there, been to university there. And yet at other times he could sound overwhelmingly Italian. Chameleon man. 'Subjects such as?'

'Sit down.' He gestured to the bench and went back inside the cabin, returning minutes later with the battered old tray which held the coffee-pot, two enamel mugs and a bowl of sugar lumps. He stirred sugar into both mugs, handed her one, then sat down beside her, his long legs in the tight faded denims stretched out in front of him, and she was achingly aware of how close he was.

'What did you want to talk about?'

'We have to discuss what we plan to do if you *are* pregnant.'

She felt like an inconvenience he couldn't wait to be rid of. 'Go ahead,' she said. 'I'm all ears.'

'Well, for a start—we're not talking hypotheticals any more, are we, Cressida? According to what you told the doctor—your period is three days late.'

'Yes,' she answered dully, anticipating with dread what his response was going to be.

She heard him swear softly beneath his breath, saw

a brief fire light the dark eyes. 'You're pregnant, aren't you?' he whispered. 'You must be. You're never late.'

And those few words battered her even more than others which had gone before. How well he knew her—every mood, every stage of the cycle that made her a woman. Only the secret that she still loved him, which was locked inside her heart, remained a mystery to him.

'Are you?' he persisted.

She shook her head. 'No, I'm never late.'

His hand went out as if to touch her, but she instinctively flinched, crying out for and yet terrified of the contact. He saw the movement and his face hardened, the hand going to rest in the pocket of his jeans, pulling the denim tight over the hard lines of his thighs.

She tried to keep her voice calm; earlier protestations aside, a baby deserved more than being subjected to endless waves of stress from its mother. 'And you're right, of course. What we have to decide now is what we're going to do about it.'

He looked at her steadily. 'We could live together.'

She thought she must have misheard him. 'What?'

'We could live together,' he repeated. 'Have the baby, and stay with me.'

It was like some horrible nightmare, like some quasi marriage proposal, and the calculating, businesslike way in which he spoke made it a cruel parody of the first time he had proposed to her. 'What do you mean?' she asked tremulously,

'It is the only solution. For you know me well enough, *cara*, to know that I would allow no child of mine to be brought up as a *bastardo*.' He bit the word out, centuries of aristocratic pride harshly distorting his voice. 'Or by another man. You know that, don't you?'

Yes, she knew that. 'But I don't understand—how would we...?'

He stared at her consideringly. 'We will not make the mistakes of the past. You will have all the freedom you require to pursue your career, but you will base your life with me, and the baby. You have seen how it is possible for us to live in comparative harmony, and, for the sake of our child, we will continue to strive for such harmony.'

In a minute she would wake up. 'It sounds so cold-blooded,' she whispered, remembering the words of love which had accompanied the first proposal. 'More like a business arrangement than anything else.'

'But that is precisely what it will be, Cressida.' There was a hint of wry irony in his voice as he stared at her. 'Many good marriages have started in just such a way. And let us not forget,' he finished bitterly, 'we did not do so well before, in the hot-blooded way.'

The cruelly dispassionate way in which he spoke was turning the blood in her veins to ice. 'But what about—about—' She faltered to find the right words, her cheeks flushed with the awful irony of it all.

'Sex?' he inserted, hateful humour at her discomfort dancing in his eyes. 'Is that what you mean but are afraid to say, *cara*?'

She strove to maintain a hold on this crazy reality. 'What kind of marriage did you have in mind, Stefano?'

His eyes were hooded, and for the first time he touched her, his hand going out to cup her chin in his palm, forcing her to stare into the dark, velvety eyes.

'That is your choice, *cara*,' he said softly. 'And yours alone. You know how much I want you. And I think that you have demonstrated quite graphically that the feeling is reciprocal.'

Shock waves of self-disgust rippled through her. 'You—bastard,' she hissed. 'You out and out bastard,' and her fists went up to flail against his chest, but he captured her wrists, lying them both over the frantic hammering of his heart.

'Is the truth so very painful, Cressida?' he murmured softly. 'Mmm?'

And as she stared into the dark face she recognised the honesty behind his words. He had stripped her bare of her defences, had seen behind the façade of feigned dislike, to recognise the burning need she still had for him. And how it would amuse him to discover that her need went far deeper than mere physical fulfilment—that she was still in love with him.

'So what is your answer to be, *cara*? Will you stay here with me? As my wife?'

She pulled her hands away from him. 'And what if I refuse?'

His face became a cold mask. 'If you refuse I shall fight you, and I think you know I will win,' he said ruthlessly. 'An actress, with no means of support— what could you offer my child? No court of law in the world would award you custody.'

'You seem to have it all worked out,' she said woodenly, but he surprised her then by pulling her into his arms, and her traitorous body melted against him even as she put up a half-hearted attempt to struggle away from him.

'I gave you the worst possible scenario,' he said into

the softness of her hair. 'Because you asked. But I do not want that, *cara*. I want you here, as mother to my child. As wife to me. I think it can work.' His voice hardened. 'We will *make* it work.'

She closed her eyes, giving in to the urge to lean fully into his arms, the hand caressing her back, washing every objection out of her head.

'So will you agree, Cressida?' he asked, with quiet confidence.

She felt his hand move down to rest in the hollow of her waist and it felt so right to have him hold her that way that all the fight went out of her. It was too hard to fight him, but even harder to fight herself.

She kept her head buried in his chest, unwilling to let him see how her eyes were pleading for soft words from him. 'Very well, Stefano,' she said quietly. 'I will stay with you.'

'Excellent.' His voice blazed with triumph, and his mouth came down to claim hers with a fire which knocked her senseless. For a moment she tried to resist the gentle pressure of his lips, but it was no good at all; her body was betraying her as it had done so many times in the past and she began to melt with the slow, familiar fire of arousal.

'Cressida.' He spoke the word against her mouth, his hands moving from her hair to curve themselves over her hips, gently pulling her against him, so that she was moulded into him, her softness against his hardness.

She was drowning in the insistent sweetness of his kiss, but as she became aware of his growing arousal, the hardness straining and pushing against the taut material of his jeans, then alarm bells began to ring inside her head. She wanted him, yes, and needed him at that moment—as perhaps she had never needed him before. As if, by making love to her, he might fill some of the aching emptiness inside her.

But not here, she could not let him take her here, not when she remembered what it *had* been like, when there had been love, not bad blood between them. And if her love had stood the test of time, his had not, and it would mock her, kill her to allow his heartless possession of her, here, where she had once had all of him.

With a monumental effort she pulled away from him, saw his eyes narrow with disbelief.

'*Cara*?' he murmured huskily.

She shook her head, backing away from him, afraid that if he touched her again she would be lost. 'I can't, Stefano. Not now. Not like this.'

It was as if she had doused him with icy water, for the passion left his face instantly. 'Such sensibilities!' he mocked. 'A little too basic for you, is it, *cara*? Your tastes have grown more sophisticated, it seems. Do I take it that you would prefer the comfort of the villa?'

She stood up quickly. 'I just want to get out of here,' she said, in a voice which she strove to prevent from breaking, but he caught her by the arm, the dark eyes boring into her as they studied her.

'Understand this, Cressida,' he said softly. 'I am not a man to beg, and I will not beg you to have sex with me. And if you can't be honest about your own needs—well...' His eyes glittered. 'I will only wait so long. Believe it. This marriage will only work if we are honest with one another.'

She thought about his words all the way back to the

villa. He had spoken about honesty, and yet she *dared* not be honest with him, for if she did that then wouldn't it expose the laughably unequal balance of affection? But if she had agreed to stay with him, then what was the point of fighting him? Better, surely, to enter into this strange marriage wholeheartedly. Stefano would be a good father, she knew that with a blinding certainty, and stranger things had happened. Couldn't they work on the common bond which the baby would undoubtedly provide?

At the door of the villa, he spoke. 'So will you be down for supper tonight?'

It was, she thought, what they called a loaded question. Her agreement would tell him a lot more than whether or not she was dining with him. 'Yes, Stefano. I will.'

He nodded. 'Good. And please think about what I have said.'

But I have done, she thought, as she made her way to her room, marvelling at the shiver of anticipation which lightened her footsteps.

Tonight, she thought, as she stood beneath the jets of the shower. Tonight they would begin again. And she would do everything in her power to make the baby bring them together as babies sometimes could. Was that naïve, or true?

She took great care in dressing her hair and choosing her gown, finally deciding on a pale lemon silk. She slid the side zip up in one fluid movement and stepped back to survey the results in the long mirror, when her hand clutched on to the dressing-table, her white face staring back at her in disbelief as a horribly familiar cramp clasped stone fingers around her womb.

*   *   *

'So you see,' Cressida's voice was very steady, 'there was no need to make any plans, after all. It was a false alarm. I expect,' her voice rushed on a little now, 'that it was all the strain that made my period late. It's lucky, really, isn't it?' she asked brightly, hopelessly praying for his denial.

'Lucky?' he echoed, his back to her. 'Indeed,' he said quietly.

One word. That was all it would have taken. One little word which he now had no reason to say. Stay.

Keep calm, she thought. Only a little bit longer and then you can cry as much as you like. 'So of course there's no reason for me to stay. Not now.'

'Of course,' he echoed again.

'And I really will have to get back to London, start looking for work, and—'

'Cressida,' he turned round then, meeting her gaze for the first time since she'd told him that there would be no baby, 'are you—sorry?' His eyes searched her face. 'About the baby?'

If she had to go, then it would be with dignity. Why make Stefano privy to the heartache which was tearing at her soul? 'I think it was probably for the best,' she answered quietly, remembering the anguished sob which had been torn from her throat as she'd sighted the first spot of blood.

'I see.' He spoke with cool dispassion, as if someone had just told him that it had stopped raining.

There was nothing to see in his face. Nothing at all. This, she thought, was Stefano at his most enigmatic, and she had to get out of here before she disintegrated before him. 'I'd like to leave as soon as possible.'

There was a long silence, but when he spoke it was

still in that curious emotionless voice. 'I'll have a plane chartered for first thing tomorrow morning—'

'No, Stefano.' She shook her head. 'I—don't want a private jet.' With him at her side, perhaps, forcing her to endure even more hours of pretending that she didn't care? 'I'd like to fly home with one of the airlines, please. Alone.'

His mouth twisted at the sides as he stared back at her. 'As you wish,' he said abruptly. 'I will see to it immediately.' And he turned and left the room.

She couldn't face supper, and fled to her room, enduring the longest night of her life as she tried to envisage a future which would no longer include him.

Morning arrived, and Cressida quickly dressed. In the dining-room, all laid up for breakfast, she came across Rosa, an unusually subdued Rosa, pale beneath the olive skin, and Cressida bit her lip, holding on to her own composure with difficulty. She refused bread and fruit and poured herself a large cup of strong black coffee.

'Has Stefano already had breakfast?'

Rosa shook her head. 'None of you is hungry this morning,' she said pointedly.

'And where is he now?'

'The *signore* went out very early. He did not say where.'

'But I'm supposed to be flying to England this morning.'

Rosa nodded. 'Yes, *signora*—he told me. He has left the ticket for you in his study. He said the driver will collect you at eleven.'

Cressida put her cup back in the saucer, staring at Rosa, scarcely believing what she heard, knowing that she had to ask the question. 'Isn't he coming back, then?' To say goodbye?

Rosa looked embarrassed. 'No, *signora*,' she said quietly.

And that was how much she meant to him. He had left without even the courtesy of a farewell. She found the ticket on his desk, mocking her in its isolation. A solitary plane ticket lying on a desk. No note, no nothing. She felt the tears well up in her eyes, and she blinked them back. Just hold on, she told herself. Hold on until you get back to England.

It was all like some dreadful nightmare which she somehow had to get through, saying goodbye to Rosa, who was openly distressed, and then the villa growing smaller and smaller as they drove away, her stupid heart lurching with disappointment when she realised that Stefano really *wasn't* even going to say goodbye to her.

At Rome airport, bustling as always, she quickly checked in. She looked at her watch—she had about an hour to kill, and she couldn't bear to go and sit idly in the departure lounge with nothing to do but torture herself with thoughts of Stefano. She would go and look in some of the small shops in the airport at clothes she had no intention of buying.

But the first shop she came to was a baby boutique and she found herself picking up one of the impossibly tiny little garments and holding it up to the light. What would their future have been like if she *had* been pregnant? But then her eyes filled with tears, and she half stumbled out of the shop.

'Are you all right, *signora*?' The shop assistant was staring at her with concern.

'*Sì, sì,*' she nodded. '*Grazie.*'

She came out of the shop, blinking back the tears, when she heard some kind of commotion.

'Honey, you can look but you most certainly can't touch,' came a smoky American drawl, and Cressida, remembering the voice instantly, looked up in horror to see Ebony, Stefano's Amazonian model friend, walking in her direction, swatting off a small man who scuttled beside her as if he had been a fly.

Like a rabbit transfixed by headlights, Cressida found herself unable to move, staring at the striking model. She was wearing a black leather jumpsuit, black boots and a matching black leather sombrero and she was exciting the attention of every man within eyeshot.

And suddenly Cressida understood the awful truth. Ebony here. In Rome. Had Stefano shipped her in now that his ex-wife was safely on her way? Sick inside, she shuddered. He hadn't even wasted a single day— off with the old, and on with the new.

There was no way she could face Ebony, to see triumph on her face, the knowing expression in those dark chocolate eyes only adding to her humiliation, and loss. She had half turned away when she heard the drawling voice, and there was its owner, studying her with a look of barely restrained amusement.

'Well, well, well! And who do we have here? Hi, there, Cathryn!'

'Cressida,' she corrected automatically.

The beautiful almond shaped-eyes were regarding her faded jeans and sweater with curiosity. 'So,' she drawled, 'we have the touching reconciliation.'

Cressida swayed slightly. Their reconciliation. If

Ebony began to fill her in with details of how she and Stefano were now getting together again after the false alarm...

But the dark-haired model had caught her by the forearm, as if sensing that Cressida was close to breaking point, her eyes piercing as she took in the deathly white pallor. 'Hey,' she murmured. 'Where's Stefano?'

With an effort, Cressida drew her shoulders back. What had she told herself about dignity? 'I have no idea,' she said coolly.

'Isn't he meeting you?'

The words were surprisingly easy to say. 'No, he isn't. I'm flying back to England.'

'I see.' Ebony's eyes narrowed. 'Running away again, I guess.'

'It's none of your damned—'

'Listen, Princess,' she shook her head, 'don't tell me it's none of my business. It seems to me you could do with a little straight talking. Do you want to know something? I would have done anything for Stefano. Anything. I was crazy about the guy. He could have had me, or any woman he wanted—like that!' She snapped her fingers. 'But he didn't. Wanna know why?'

'I don't think I—'

Ebony bent forward, the black hair splaying silkily all over her shoulders. 'Because he's still in love with you, you numbskull!'

Cressida stared at Ebony in disbelief. 'You don't know what you're talking about.'

'Oh, don't I? Well, how's this for size? You don't deserve a man like Stefano, honey. If I had a man like

that in love with me, you could take my job and jump
up and down on it, and dump it in the garbage.'

Reality was becoming more elusive by the second.
'Stefano isn't in love with me,' she said dully.

'Oh, *please*! The guy's so hung up on you he can't
think straight. Surely,' she stared at Cressida, 'you
knew *that*?'

Cressida shook her head. 'You're mistaken.'

But suddenly Ebony was grinning, as if she were
secretly enjoying some hugely amusing private joke.
'Well, don't just take my word for it, honey,' she
drawled. 'I guess there's someone here you just might
believe!' Her eyes were looking over Cressida's shoulder.

'Cressida,' said a soft, deep voice.

She turned round as if in slow motion, not believing
that it could be true. But it was. Stefano, his eyes
scrutinising her.

'But—' she stammered, when there was yet another
commotion.

'Ebony—*honey*! Will you stick close to me, for
God's sake? I *have* got the tickets, after all!'

Six feet six inches of blond, tanned, all-American
male strode over to Ebony, and clasped her leather-
covered arm possessively.

Ebony stared back up at him, like a child on
Christmas morning. 'Hi, Clinton,' she smiled, batting
her eyelashes outrageously. 'I knew you'd find me.'
She swivelled her hand up underneath Clinton's arm.
'Come on, honey, these two have a little bit of sorting
out to do!' And she began to pull a bewildered-looking
Clinton away, but as they passed she dipped her head
to Cressida's ear. 'To tell the truth,' she whispered, 'I

never really went for that dark, moody, broody type!' And then she was gone.

The two of them stood staring at one another. The airport sounds retreated as she drowned in the intensity of his gaze, frightened that the tenuous dreams which Ebony's words had given birth to were about to be smashed.

'Why are you here?' she whispered.

'Because I couldn't bear to let you go. Not a second time. Whatever it takes to make you stay—I'll do it.'

Some distant part of her was aware that people were looking at them, but she didn't care. 'Why?' Another small word. Her future depending on the answer.

'Because I love you,' he said, very softly. 'I love you, Cressida, as I've never loved a woman before, and will never love again—God help me!'

And she burst into tears.

'Cressida!' He had caught her to his chest, kissing the top of her head, his arms encircling her in a strong warm embrace she never wanted to leave. '*Cara! Cara! Mia cara*—please don't cry.' And he cupped her chin in his hand, forcing her face upwards to stare at him.

'Listen to me,' he said urgently. 'I've been the world's biggest fool.' He shook his head slowly from side to side as he looked down at her. 'When I received that damned letter from your solicitor, I knew that it was almost too late. That in my arrogance and my pride I'd allowed things to drift for so long.' The dark eyes glittered. 'I knew I had to see you again— so I persuaded the original backers of your play to pull out and let me take over.

'Nothing had changed. Not a thing. I loved you as

much as ever. But I knew that I had to tread carefully, if I was to stand any chance after the way I'd behaved towards you.' He sighed. 'I wanted to tell you how I felt the first time I saw you again—but I was afraid that I might frighten you off. *Dio!* It was hard. When I saw you in Adrian's arms, even on stage, it was as much as I could do not to tear the theatre apart with my bare hands. But I was determined not to let it show.

'And so I played it cool, until the last night of the play. God knows, I didn't mean to risk making you pregnant, but in a way fate played into my hands. And it gave me the opportunity to bring you here with me...'

'But you let me leave this morning?' She stared up at him and flinched at the naked pain which clouded the dark eyes.

'I was in shock,' he said quietly. 'Despairing. I had wanted there to be our baby. Prayed for it. So much. So I left the villa early this morning and walked and walked. And then I came to my senses. I thought—I cannot let her go. Not again. I have to tell her what I feel. How much I love her.'

She bent her head forward to lean on his chest. 'Why on earth didn't you tell me?' she asked, her voice muffled against the dampness of his shirt. 'In all the time I've been here, you've never mentioned the word love to me.'

'Love?' He looked down at her then, his finger lifting her chin, his eyes sad as they surveyed her. 'In the past we talked of love, but discussed nothing else. Words of love are easy to say—but this time I thought that I would show you, and that perhaps one day you could learn to love me again. And, *mia cara*, I intend to do that. Whatever it takes—I'm going to make you love me.'

A tremulous smile lifted the wide mouth. 'But I do love you, Stefano,' she said, her calm tone doing nothing to disguise the slight shake of emotion behind her words. 'I never stopped loving you.'

The dark eyes blazed. 'Don't play games with me, Cressida. Not now. I can't take it.'

She marvelled at the vulnerability she saw written in his face. 'I love you,' she repeated.

He stared at her for a long, hard moment, as if seeking the truth in the green eyes which returned his gaze so steadily, and then, with a small, strangled sound at the back of his throat, he caught her to him, and suddenly he was kissing her with a fierce hunger which sent her senses spinning.

It seemed a long time later when he looked down at her. 'Oh, *cara*,' he whispered. 'Where did we go so wrong?'

She stared up at him, trying to put it into words. 'You were so strong, so important, so powerful—and I felt swamped. I felt as though everyone disapproved when we came here at weekends—your family, the servants—not understanding why you'd married this young foreigner who never fitted in. And you never wanted to discuss it—you always grew so tight-lipped. So my work became like a kind of refuge, I suppose. It gave me back the self-esteem I thought I'd lost. And you resented it. That's why—that's why when you told me to choose between my work and you...' Her voice died away.

He nodded. 'I know. It put you in an impossible

situation. And then it became a matter of pride, with neither one of us wanting to back down.' He shook his head. 'So many misunderstandings.'

'I used to dread coming to the villa,' she confessed. 'I felt as if you were ashamed of me. The way you used to make us leave dinner parties early, when I tried to speak Italian.'

'*Dio!*' he swore softly. 'Do you know why I did that? I hated the way that no one gave you a chance when you were trying so hard. I refused to have them treating you that way.'

'We should have talked about it.'

His face was full of rueful acceptance. 'But I was not a man to talk. Brought up to be strong, as someone for the family to lean on—I felt I had to be strong for you, too. That maybe by not making an issue of it, by *ignoring* what was happening, if you like—that the problems would just go away.' He smiled at her tenderly. 'Do you remember—that first time when I took you out again in London?'

She nodded, remembering the tense meal with David there.

'We were in the restaurant, and you spoke to the waiter in Italian. I was amazed. I thought that your experiences here would have made you want to forget every word you'd ever learnt.'

She shook her head. 'Never.'

He bent his head to speak softly in her ear. 'I love you, Cressida, do you know that? Always. And in future we talk. No secrets. OK?'

'OK,' she whispered, her voice breaking with emotion as he pressed the palm of her hand to his lips.

* * *

A week later she awoke in his bed, moonlight streaming in over the crumpled sheets, his dark limbs interlocking with hers, the crisp hairs of his torso tickling the breasts which were jutting against his chest. His hand was idly massaging the back of her neck, and he smiled when she turned to him.

'Was that *"nice"*?' he mocked her.

She stretched her body with languid pleasure. 'I could think of some far more appropriate descriptions than "nice",' she told him, feeling him begin to harden in response to her words.

'That's how you described that night at your flat, *mia cara*,' his hand moving from her neck to trace tiny circles on the satin skin above her breasts.

'That's because I thought you were indifferent to me,' she said softly. 'The same way that I put your absence this morning when I left down to indifference that I was leaving.'

'Crazy woman,' he chided, and his face grew serious. 'I couldn't face seeing you go. The end to all my dreams of a reconciliation. I thought you couldn't wait to get away.'

'And I thought that now there was no longer going to be the chance of a baby you would want me to go away.'

He lowered his head to kiss her lips with soft precision. 'Speaking of babies...' he murmured, then halted when he saw the protestation in her eyes. 'And yes, you, my beautiful Cressida, can choose where we live, which nanny you would like—I intend to make it as easy as I can for you to follow your career.'

She shook her head. 'I'd like a baby, but perhaps in a year or two—maybe I'd like you to myself for a bit first.' She lay her head down on his chest. 'And as for nannies, well, we'll see when the time comes. Maybe I'll feel like taking a year or two off,' her green eyes sparkled with pleasure. 'Getting to know our baby.' She looked up at him, a question in her eyes.

'What?'

She shook her head. It was much too painful. 'It doesn't matter.'

'No secrets,' he reminded her, bending his head to kiss her bare shoulder.

She bit her lip. 'It's about Ebony,' she said.

A spark of amusement lit his eyes. 'Ah, Ebony,' he smiled. 'You want me to tell you that there was nothing between us, that I never made love to her—'

'No, stop it!' She started to turn away from him, her face burning with jealous rage, but he stopped her, lying her on her back and moving above her.

'But it's true, *cara*,' he told her softly, and she looked into his eyes and read the truth there. 'I *wanted* to want Ebony, but I couldn't. Every time I ever looked at another woman, all I saw was you. We were simply "just good friends"—that is all. Ebony was a good listener.'

'Because—?'

He nodded. 'She listened because she was in love with me,' he said gently. 'When I realised that, we stopped seeing one another.'

'I like her,' she said suddenly, realising that it was true. 'I—oh, Stefano...' He was no longer stroking the skin above her breast but was moving in tantalising caresses around the pink-tipped nub itself, and as his mouth took over from his fingers she wriggled with pleasure.

He raised his dark head and grinned, one hand sliding with agonising slowness up her naked thigh. 'What, *mia cara*?' he whispered. 'What is it?'

She wanted to tell him how much she loved him, but the words seemed suddenly unimportant, and she gave herself up to his kiss, her body telling him all he needed to know.

The world's bestselling romance series.

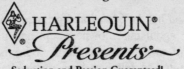

HARLEQUIN®
Presents

Seduction and Passion Guaranteed!

Introducing Jane Porter's exciting new series

**The Galván men: proud Argentine aristocrats…
who've chosen American rebels as their brides!**

IN DANTE'S DEBT
Harlequin Presents #2298

Count Dante Galván was ruthless—and though it broke Daisy's heart she had no alternative but to hand over control of her family's stud farm to him. She was in Dante's debt up to her ears! Daisy knew she was far too ordinary ever to become the count's wife— but could she resist his demands that she repay her dues in his bed?

On sale January 2003

LAZARO'S REVENGE
Harlequin Presents #2304

Lazaro Herrera has vowed revenge on Dante, his half brother, who refuses to acknowledge his existence. When Dante's sister-in-law Zoe arrives in Argentina, it seems the perfect opportunity. But the clash of Zoe's blond and blue-eyed beauty with his own smoldering dark looks creates a sexual force so strong that Lazaro's plan begins to fall apart….

On sale February 2003

**Pick up a Harlequin Presents® novel and you will enter
a world of spine-tingling passion and
provocative, tantalizing romance!**

Available wherever Harlequin books are sold.

HARLEQUIN®
Makes any time special ®

Visit us at www.eHarlequin.com

HPGALVAN

International bestselling author

SANDRA MARTON

invites you to attend the

WEDDING *of the* YEAR

Glitz and glamour prevail in this volume
containing a trio of stories in which
three couples meet at a
high society wedding—and
soon find themselves
walking down the aisle!

Look for it in November 2002.

HARLEQUIN®
Makes any time special ®